TEMPTATION IN PARADISE

BY
JOANNA NEIL

All rights reserved including the right of reproduction in whole or in part in any form. This edition is published by arrangement with Harlequin Books S.A.

This is a work of fiction. Names, characters, places, locations and incidents are purely fictional and bear no relationship to any real life individuals, living or dead, or to any actual places, business establishments, locations, events or incidents. Any resemblance is entirely coincidental.

This book is sold subject to the condition that it shall not, by way of trade or otherwise, be lent, resold, hired out or otherwise circulated without the prior consent of the publisher in any form of binding or cover other than that in which it is published and without a similar condition including this condition being imposed on the subsequent purchaser.

® and TM are trademarks owned and used by the trademark owner and/or its licensee. Trademarks marked with ® are registered with the United Kingdom Patent Office and/or the Office for Harmonisation in the Internal Market and in other countries.

Published in Great Britain 2015
by Mills & Boon, an imprint of Harlequin (UK) Limited,
Eton House, 18-24 Paradise Road, Richmond, Surrey, TW9 1SR

© 2015 Joanna Neil

ISBN: 978-0-263-24688-9

Harlequin (UK) Limited's policy is to use papers that are natural, renewable and recyclable products and made from wood grown in sustainable forests. The logging and manufacturing processes conform to the legal environmental regulations of the country of origin.

Printed and bound in Spain
by CPI, Barcelona

Dear Reader

Wouldn't it be wonderful to escape to a Caribbean paradise island? Imagine it: palm-fringed beaches, turquoise lagoons, hummingbirds sipping honey from deep-throated flowers. We could leave our troubles behind and indulge our dreams in this idyllic place.

Or could we?

That's exactly what Jessie hopes to do when she leaves the UK for warmer shores, but things turn out to be not quite so peaceful in paradise as she might have hoped for.

Trouble seems to follow her brother around, for one thing, and her father adds his two-pennyworth, but the biggest headache of all comes in the form of a heartbreaker doctor who seems to have his sights firmly fixed on her.

Will Jessie and José manage to sort out their problems? Well, this *is* a magical island, after all…

With love

Joanna

Recent titles by Joanna Neil:

DARING TO DATE HER BOSS
A DOCTOR TO REMEMBER
SHELTERED BY HER TOP-NOTCH BOSS
RETURN OF THE REBEL DOCTOR
HIS BRIDE IN PARADISE
TAMED BY HER BROODING BOSS
DR RIGHT ALL ALONG

**These books are also available in eBook format
from www.millsandboon.co.uk**

CHAPTER ONE

'I'M REALLY GLAD you decided to come out to the Caribbean, Jessie.'

Ben raised his voice above the sound of merrymaking going on inside the house immediately behind them, and for a moment or two his expression was solemn.

'I didn't expect you to come, you know—it must have taken a lot of sorting out and I feel really bad about pouring out my troubles to you and putting pressure on you that way. I shouldn't have done it.'

He pressed his lips together in a rueful grimace.

'You had enough on your plate back in London, and I know I ought to have kept things to myself, but I wasn't thinking properly. I just needed to talk to you. Somehow, you always manage to make me feel better when I'm at my lowest.'

Jessie reached for his hand. 'You're my brother,' she said softly. 'I'll always be there for you. You can depend on it.'

He gave her fingers an answering squeeze. 'I'll do the same for you, Jessie. You'll see.'

'I know you will,' she said.

They were sitting on the terrace of a beautiful house, facing the sea, the darkness lit by flickering golden light from tiki torches planted at intervals along the paths and among the shrubbery. French doors opened out on to the patio to let the balmy tropical air circulate through the house, and in the background the heavy, rhythmic sound of steel drums beat out a lively calypso melody.

Inside the house, people were dancing, just as Jessie had been doing a short while ago with a number of eager partners. She hadn't taken any of them up on their pleas for future romantic dates. Having her fingers burned back home had been warning enough and she wasn't looking to get caught out that way again. As for the rest of the partygoers, they were chatting or helping themselves to the delicious food that had been set out on the island bar in the kitchen.

For now, though, Jessie just wanted to breathe in the night air and spend some time with her brother.

'I feel as though I've landed in paradise,' she said, sighing with contentment. 'The island is incredible, fantastic. And as for this house, it's so lovely—the owner must be very trusting to allow your friends to throw a party here while he's away.'

'I suppose so.' Ben frowned, as though he hadn't thought about it before now. 'Anyway, Zach and Eric said they had his blessing. But, then, we've been renovating the place for him for the last couple of weeks—he let us have the keys so we could come and go as we pleased. I think he probably knows by now that we can be trusted.'

'I guess so.' She was puzzled. 'Is that how long you've worked for him—a couple of weeks?' It didn't seem long enough for a man to decide he could safely leave his home in the hands of strangers.

'Yes. I had to find work quickly after Dad kicked me out, and they needed an extra man on the team to do the labouring. Dr Benitez—the owner—already knew me because I've been helping out with the diving for the coral reef study alongside him in my spare time, so he set me on. He said I could do some work on his other properties when the renovations here were finished. He has a building company and rents out the properties once they've been brought up to a good standard.'

'It's good you were able to find something so soon.' It sounded as though his new employer, Dr Benitez, was a wealthy, powerful individual—some kind of marine biologist who also had a property portfolio. It was good that Ben had landed on his feet.

She looked at her brother. He was barely nineteen, well muscled and fit from working out, but his appearance disguised the fact that he was young for his years and was still racked by the legacy of a troubled childhood. Of course, they'd both been affected by the break-up of their parents' marriage, but Ben had only been eleven when it had happened, and his whole world had been turned upside down. Perhaps Jessie, being a few years older, had managed to handle the situation better.

Their mother had been devastated by the divorce, and had retreated into a world of her own, leaving Jessie, seventeen years old at the time, to do what she could to take care of her brother and support him emotionally. She'd carried on doing that while she'd been at medical school, being able to go on living at home to care for him and her mother, but for a long time Ben had struggled. He'd tried desperately to hold on to the image of a father figure, but it had all been in vain. In the end his hopes had been dashed, leaving him confused and more than a little rebellious. This latest attempt to bond with his father by coming out to the Caribbean had also turned sour.

Now, though, the fact that Jessie was here with him had obviously lifted his spirits and had allowed him to put his troubles behind him for a while.

'You should try this rum punch, Jessie,' he said cheerfully. There was an ice bucket on the white-painted ornamental garden table and he lifted the lid and used tongs to scoop out some ice cubes, dropping them into a tall glass. Then he picked up a jug and poured bright amber-coloured liquid over the ice. 'I'm sure you'll like it.' He handed her the glass. 'It's a favourite round here.' He watched her, his youthful, handsome face expectant.

'Thanks…' Her mouth curved. 'Though I think I may be getting near to my limit already. There was the wine, earlier…and—oh—the mojitos…' She rolled her eyes in recollection of a great experience. But perhaps she'd overdone the alcohol a bit?

All the same, Jessie put the glass to her lips and sipped slowly, savouring the flavours on her tongue and trying to pick out the different ingredients. There was rum, of course, a dash of lime juice, sweet syrup and orange… and maybe a hint of Angostura bitters.

'Mmm…you're right,' she murmured. 'This is just what I needed.' Warmth slowly curled and settled in her abdomen and she smiled up at him. 'I think this is the first time I've been able to truly unwind since I stepped off the plane yesterday.'

Ben nodded, pleased, and leaned back in his chair. 'You'll love it here. The change will do you good.'

'Yes…I hope so.'

She looked around, sipping her drink as she absorbed the flawless, landscaped surroundings. The heady, sweet scent of frangipani filled the air, and in the pools of light spread by the torches she could see exotic blooms of bougainvillea, their magenta bracts circling tiny white flowers and next to them a mass of bright pink hibiscus.

He smiled. 'It's a great party, isn't it? It's amazing what you can pull together at the last minute…and the food's fantastic. Would you like me to get you some more of those jerk chicken wraps that you liked earlier—and maybe some rice?'

'That sounds lovely—but I can get them for myself,' she said with a smile, starting to get to her feet.

'No, no…you stay there and relax. You're probably still suffering from jet lag. Enjoy the scenery.'

He left her, walking towards the open patio doors, and Jessie subsided back into her chair, watching the moonlit waves of the Caribbean breaking over smooth white sand. Palm fronds bent in the gentle breeze, outlined against the clear night sky.

She stretched lazily, crossing one palely bronzed leg over the other. The warm tropical air caressed her bare shoulders and she sighed contentedly. This was true bliss. Perhaps she should have done this long ago, put the house up for rental and left all her cares behind her.

'Perhaps I could get you another drink?' Coming from close by, the male voice startled her. It was faintly accented—a Spanish inflection, perhaps?—deep and husky, wrapping itself around her senses and sending an unexpected thrill of anticipation to run up and down her spine. She sat up, alert, her skin prickling.

'I…um…' She looked up at the man who seemed to have appeared out of nowhere and who was now standing by her side. Her heartbeat quickened. He was dark and mysterious in the shadowy light, tall and immaculately dressed in beautifully tailored trousers and a midnight-blue linen shirt. 'Thanks, but…er…I'm not sure if I should. I think I might have had enough to drink already.' Her head felt warm and fuzzy, a sure sign the alcohol was hitting the spot.

He smiled. 'Maybe one more won't hurt if you eat some food. Your friend has gone to fetch it, I think.'

'Your friend,' he'd said. She pondered that for a moment and he must have taken her silence for acquiescence because he started to top up her glass.

'He—uh—he's—' She broke off, wondering how long he'd been standing there. 'I didn't see you come out onto the terrace,' she murmured, 'or hear you, for that matter.'

He gave a wry smile. 'That's not surprising really, with the music going at full blast in there.' He nodded towards the house. 'But actually I came from around the side of the building.'

'Oh, I see.' She frowned. That would explain why she hadn't seen him before this. He hadn't been at the party until now. 'Are you a neighbour?' A sudden thought struck her. 'Have you come to complain about the noise?' The beach houses were some distance apart, but sound probably carried quite a way out here in the tropics. 'I'm sorry if it's been disturbing you.'

His expression was wry. 'It certainly caught my attention.'

'Oh…yes…of course. Well, I'm sure we can get them to turn it down a few notches, though I imagine things will be winding up here before too long.' She made a face. 'It's very late and some of us have places to be in the morning.'

'That's very true.' He looked at her thoughtfully, an appreciative glint sparking in his blue eyes. 'Though I must say there are some things that are definitely worth staying up for.' His glance drifted over her, making her hotly aware of the clothes she was wearing, party clothes, very different from what she might have worn back in London. Her strapless top clung to her curves like a second skin and her short sarong-style skirt wrapped itself lovingly around her hips and left a good deal of bare leg on show.

'I…uh…' Unsettled by his intent scrutiny, she stood up. 'Perhaps I should go and see about quietening things down a bit?'

He shook his head. 'Leave it to me—I'll sort it out.' There was a slight edge to his voice as he added, 'There are certain people I need to see.' But then he relaxed and said softly, 'For the moment, I'd much sooner have you stay here and talk to me.'

He studied her once more, his gaze moving slowly over her as though he couldn't quite tear himself away. His glance lingered for a moment or two on the burnished chestnut hair falling in silky waves below her shoulders, and then his gaze wandered over her slender figure, leaving a trail of heat in its wake.

Colour rose in her cheeks. 'I suppose that would be all right.'

'I'm glad.' He moved a little closer to her and all her senses erupted and began to clamour for attention. Warning bells sounded dimly in her head, but she ignored them. After all, what could be the harm in talking to him? 'I didn't mean to eavesdrop,' he said, 'but I couldn't help overhearing that you might be suffering from jet lag. Have you come far? Are you here for a holiday?'

'Not a holiday, no…though I'll admit I wouldn't mind a few days soaking up the sun and exploring the island. I'm usually a hard worker, always on the go, but I have to say, as soon as I arrived here something made me want to give up on the idea of doing anything strenuous. Everyone's so laid back…the pace is so relaxed.' She smiled. 'From the little I've seen, it's beautiful here…very different from London, where I've been living.'

'It is.' He sent her a quizzical look. 'So, if you're not here for a holiday…?'

She shook her head, causing her silky chestnut curls

to ripple and settle once more over her bare shoulders. 'I managed to organise some temporary work—I'll be over here for three months, working as a doctor in the paediatric emergency unit at the hospital. It isn't a full-time position, so I might need to look for something else to keep me going, but it was too good an opportunity to miss.' There would be some on-call work outside the hospital, as she understood it, and that suited her perfectly.

She shrugged lightly and his glance flicked to the creamy softness of her skin. 'It…uh…it suited me to leave the UK right now,' she went on. 'I wanted to gain a bit more experience before I decide what specialty I want to follow.'

He raised a dark brow. 'You've travelled a long way to do that.'

'Yes, that's true.' Her mouth moved awkwardly. 'Actually, I have family over here—my father has a stake in a rum distillery on the island. We haven't seen a lot of each other over the years and I thought this would give me a chance to spend some time with him.'

He frowned. 'And your mother? Is she not living here?'

She pulled in a quick breath before answering him. 'No. My parents haven't been together for quite some time. My mother died back in the UK a couple of years ago.'

'I'm sorry.' Again there was that deep Spanish inflection. His eyes darkened with compassion. 'That must have been hard for you.'

She nodded and sought to change the subject before her emotions got the better of her. Her feelings about her mother's death were still quite raw, and as for her father—their relationship was difficult, and somehow she had to sort out a way for them to get along better.

'And you?' she asked. 'Do you live here on Saint

Helene, or are you just visiting?' She picked up her glass and began to sip the rum punch he'd poured for her. Perhaps it was all in her mind, but it seemed as though the kick from the alcohol was giving her confidence.

'Oh, I live here,' he said, his mouth curving. 'My family made their home here several generations ago. Originally they were Spanish, but with a good deal of intermingling over the decades we've been left with a Spanish-American heritage.'

'Ah…that would explain your accent. I couldn't quite work it out at first. It's faint, but definitely there.' No matter how hard she tried to convince herself she was immune to any kind of male charm, his voice held a sexy, vibrant timbre that made her insides quiver. It was disturbing the way she responded to him, to say the least.

He inclined his head briefly, still holding Jessie's gaze. She was mesmerised by those dark eyes, finding it hard to break away from the intoxicating heat glinting in their depths, until a sound broke the spell and she became aware of Ben walking towards them. She didn't know whether to feel glad or let down by the interruption.

'Sorry I've been gone for so long,' Ben said, concentrating on placing a tray, laden with food, down on the table. 'I was caught up, talking to a friend from the distillery.'

'That's okay.' She put down her glass. 'I've had someone to keep me company.'

Ben straightened and for the first time looked properly at the man standing beside her. He drew in a quick breath. 'Dr Benitez…' He seemed stunned. 'I… We weren't expecting you back here for a few days. I thought your business would keep you in Florida until the end of the week.'

'I managed to complete it ahead of schedule.' The doctor's handsome sculpted features were rigid as he looked at Ben and it dawned on Jessie that something wasn't quite right here.

So this was her brother's new employer? 'You already know each other,' she said, looking from one to the other.

Ben was still caught in the searchlight of that unflinching stare. 'We do.' He gave himself a shake and made an effort to pull himself together. 'Jessie, I should introduce you… This is Dr Benitez—like I said, I've been doing some work for him this last couple of weeks.'

Jessie nodded and looked back at the doctor. 'Ben told me about the renovations he's been doing for you.' Her green eyes widened. 'Am I right in thinking this is your house?'

He nodded. 'You are.'

'Ah.' She faltered momentarily, feeling like an unwitting intruder. 'Ben told me he and his friends have been working here. It's such a lovely house—what I've seen of it so far, anyway. Which isn't a great deal,' she added hastily. 'Just the living room and kitchen and the terrace.' She didn't want him to think she'd been inspecting every nook and cranny in his absence.

'I'll be more than glad to show you the rest,' he said. His gaze was intense, heat flaring in the depths of his eyes, and her heart gave a small, involuntary leap.

'Thank you, Dr Benitez, I'd like that.'

His expression softened briefly as he looked at her. 'José…you must call me José, *chica*.'

'José.' She lowered her gaze for a second or two, a little overwhelmed by his full-on manner towards her.

'Good.'

He turned to look at Ben, and she was dismayed to see that his demeanour changed. He was entirely different in his dealings with Ben. He seemed almost hostile towards him and straight away her system went on red alert. She had to get to the root of what was wrong. 'Do you and Ben have a problem with one another?' she asked.

'I'm afraid it would seem so.' He ran his hand lightly over her elbow, sending tremors of tingling sensation to run along the length of her arm. 'Perhaps you would like to go back to the party for a few minutes?' he suggested softly. 'I need to talk to Ben in private for a moment.'

Jessie shook her head. 'I don't think so. You can say what needs to be said in front of me. I want to know what's going on.' She looked at Ben for confirmation and her brother nodded slowly, awkwardly.

'I am sorry for that,' José said. He stiffened, and turned an icy stare on Ben. 'I want to know why he thought it would be all right to hold a party in my house while I was away.' He sent her an oblique, smoky glance. 'The only point in his favour is that he brought along with him the most beautiful girl in all of Saint Helene.'

'Oh…' She was too bewildered by his condemnation of Ben to take any notice of his smooth flattery. 'You must be mistaken. I'm sure Ben wasn't the one who—'

'It's all right, Jessie. I can speak for myself.' Ben drew himself up to his full height, ready to stand up to José. 'It's not what you think, Dr Benitez. I didn't set this up.'

Jessie was floundering. Her brother couldn't have been so reckless as to arrange this party, could he? Hadn't he told her his friends, Zach and Eric, had done all the organising?

'Is that so? Really?' José raised a dark, sceptical brow. 'You're the one who has the house keys. I trusted you. Obviously I was wrong to do that.'

'But I gave the keys to Zach so we could work on the house,' Ben protested. 'He had to bring back some light fittings and cable and so on from the wholesaler when I wasn't here.'

'And you weren't here because…?'

Ben's cheeks flushed with warm colour and he averted his eyes briefly. 'I…um…Zach's an early riser but I'm never too good first thing in the morning… It just seemed better to let him do the wholesaler run. And you had given him the keys one time before you went away, so I didn't think it would matter.'

José's jaw flexed. 'What you mean to say is that you drink too much and can't get up for work on time.' His eyes were like flint. 'So Zach has the keys now?'

'Well, no…he gave them back to me tonight, just a short time ago. We've finished the work here, so he didn't need to hold on to them any more.'

Jessie's spirits sank with every word he uttered. Her brother wouldn't have organised this party, she was sure of it, but he had believed his friend when he'd said it was all right with their boss to use the house. Ben was so naive, so gullible…and now, from the look of sheer disbelief on his employer's face, she knew he was in trouble because José clearly didn't know him the way she did.

'I'll have the keys back,' José said, holding out his hand, palm upwards. 'I shall be changing the locks, of course, and installing a security system.'

Ben handed over the keys. His face was pale. 'I'm sorry, Dr Benitez,' he said. 'Really, I am. Please believe me, I didn't do this. Honestly, I thought you'd agreed to let us use the house just for tonight.'

'You seriously think I would do that?' José's stare was frosty. 'You need to start looking around for some other kind of work, Ben. I won't be needing you any more.'

Ben gave a short gasp, as though he'd been landed a blow in his midriff. 'But I didn't—honestly, I didn't do this… I wouldn't. I was wrong to let Zach have the keys, I know, but it won't happen again, I promise. I'll sort myself out. I'll be on time—I will, if you'll just give me another chance…'

José shook his head. 'You let me down and I've no wish to have my trust abused once more.'

Jessie couldn't bear to see this happening. She had to do what she could to plead her brother's case.

'José, please, won't you reconsider?' she said quietly. 'He said he didn't do this…and I believe him. Won't you give him a chance to show you that he can be trusted?'

José's features remained etched as though in stone. 'He's your *novio*, yes? You care so much for him that you would plead for him? I'm afraid your feelings for him are misplaced, *mi chica bella*.'

'No, no…you have it all wrong,' she said anxiously. 'He isn't my boyfriend—he's my brother. I know him. I understand him and I'm certain he's telling you the truth.'

José pulled in a quick breath, his eyes glittering, and for a second or two as he studied her, she dared to think that he might relent. But instead he shook his head. 'It's good that you care for your brother, Jessie, but he let me down and I believe you're letting your emotions colour your judgement. He can't be trusted to turn up for work on time and he gave my keys to a third party. He doesn't deserve your sympathy.'

'I think that's for me to decide.' Her chin jerked upwards. 'So let me get this straight…if the situation were reversed you would turn your back on a brother or a sister who needed your help?'

'I didn't say that.'

She sent him a scathing look. He had been charm itself just a short time ago, yet now he was ready to dismiss her brother without a second glance. How could she have any regard for a man who would treat her brother that way? His swift condemnation had brought all her

protective instincts to the fore, and inside she was seeth-
ing with resentment.

She'd been right to be wary of him. So much for any
expectation of good old-fashioned chivalry or plain and
simple justice.

'You haven't even bothered to check his story,' she
said tartly. 'How do you know Zach and his friend didn't
organise this?'

'Perhaps they were all in on it together. I shall have
to find out.'

His answer did nothing to appease her. She'd had
enough of this. She picked up her clutch bag from the
table and turned towards her brother. 'Come on, Ben.
We should go. We're through here. There's nothing more
to say.'

José's gaze moved over her. 'I have no argument with
you, Jessie. I would very much like you to stay.'

'And I would prefer to leave.'

Ben looked anxious, sending her a worried glance. He
bent his head towards her and said in a whisper, 'Don't
you think I should stay and help with the clearing up? I
mean, we can't leave the place like this, can we?'

'I wouldn't fret yourself about that,' she said tersely,
fully aware that José was watching them, a host of conflicting emotions written across his face. She was still
upset by his perfunctory treatment of her brother. 'Zach
and Eric can see to all that.'

'But they left half an hour ago,' Ben muttered under
his breath.

'Did they?' She gave a short laugh. 'That was conve-
nient, wasn't it? I expect they found out that Dr Benitez
had turned up. They knew they'd done wrong and they
didn't want to stay and face the consequences.'

She started to walk towards the side of the house and

after a moment's hesitation and a hasty glance in José's direction Ben hurried after her.

'Are you sure we're doing the right thing?' he persisted anxiously.

'Of course,' she said. She wouldn't be seeing Dr José Benitez again, so what did it matter? The fact that his brooding stare was burning a hole in her back only served to stiffen her resolve all the more.

CHAPTER TWO

'ARE YOU READY for your first day in the new job?' Ben refilled his coffee cup and then did the same for Jessie, sliding a mug across the breakfast table towards her.

'I think so.' Jessie gave a wry smile. 'At least, I would be if it weren't for this throbbing hangover. I knew I shouldn't have had that last drink at the party. I don't know what got into me.' Maybe it had been a nervous reaction after coming face-to-face with a man who had somehow managed to fire up all her defences.

She didn't want to dwell on the other events of the evening, but the image of the tall, dark stranger insisted on forcing its way into her mind. She'd been upset on Ben's behalf last night, but perhaps she shouldn't have reacted the way she had? After all, things might have turned out better for her brother if she'd gone on trying to appease José, instead of challenging him. She'd probably made things much worse, and now it wasn't very likely he would ever consider taking Ben on again. The pounding at her temples worsened at the thought, and she winced.

Ben helped himself to toast and spread it generously with apricot preserve. 'It was a touch of the Caribbean getting into you, I guess,' he said in a soothing tone. 'It happens to the best of us.' He watched her drizzle maple syrup on her pancake. 'Anyway, after the way things have been for you back home lately, breaking up with Lewis and all that, you probably needed to let your hair down a bit.'

'I suppose so.' She gritted her teeth, thinking about her cheating ex-boyfriend. How could she have been so blind, so trusting, not to have suspected that while she had been busy working in Accident and Emergency, Lewis had been happily making out with another woman? It had hurt badly when she'd found out the truth, and even now just thinking about it made her whole body tremble.

'You look good,' Ben said approvingly, skimming a glance over her. She was wearing a cream blouse teamed with a flower-printed skirt that fell in soft folds over her hips and a short-sleeved, matching jacket completed the ensemble. The colours were soft pastels, easy on the eye.

'I'm glad you think so.' She made an effort to pull herself together. Taking her time, she finished off the pancake and drank her coffee, then asked, 'What are you planning on doing today?'

His expression sobered. 'I'll look around for work. I have to find something as soon as possible—I can't keep sponging off you. You've helped me out more than enough already.'

'Don't worry about that. Half of the rental income from the house back home is yours by right, so that should keep you going for a bit.'

He smiled. 'Yeah, I guess. Thanks, Jessie. You're a lifesaver.'

She left the apartment a short time later and drove her hire car from the village towards the coast on the west side of the island where the hospital was situated. She was a little apprehensive about what lay ahead, starting work in an unfamiliar hospital in a foreign land, but at least for the moment she had the wonderful island scenery to help take her mind off things.

She glanced in the rear-view mirror. Behind her, the dramatic slopes of a dormant volcano dominated the island, with dense green forest carpeting the land as far as the sea's edge. In the distance a magnificent waterfall cascaded to a deep, wide rock pool and for a dreamy instant she wished she could be there, simply taking in the view.

The sheer beauty of her surroundings helped to calm her and she purposely tried to breathe in deeply. It was all so different from what she had known before... It was awe-inspiring and invigorating, and by the time she'd parked her car outside Mount Saint Helene Hospital, she felt much better able to face up to this new test.

The hospital was a neat, white-painted, two-storey building with a veranda running along one side where patients and their relatives could sit awhile in the warm air. Palm trees provided a modicum of shelter, and the grounds had been planted with yucca and brightly flowering hibiscus.

Jessie pushed open the wide main door and went inside the air-conditioned building, going over to the reception desk.

'Hello, I'm Dr Heywood,' she told the clerk. 'I'm starting work in the paediatric accident and emergency unit this morning.'

'Oh, hello, there,' the woman said, with a welcoming smile. 'It's good to see you. I'm sure you'll enjoy your time here with us. You'll find everyone very friendly and helpful.' She called over a young medic who happened to be walking by the desk. 'Hi, Dr Lombard, do you think you could show Dr Heywood the way to children's A and E? It's her first day here with us.'

'I'd be glad to. I'm headed over there now.' Dr Lombard was a good-looking young man, olive-skinned, with black hair and grey eyes. He wore tailored trousers topped by a palely striped shirt and a subtly patterned tie.

He smiled and put out a hand to Jessie, grasping her fingers warmly in his. 'I'm Robert,' he said. 'If you have any problems or queries, just ask. I expect it will all feel a bit strange to you for the first few days, but we'll look after you.'

'Thanks.' She introduced herself. 'I'm Jessie.'

She was hoping there would be time for her to get used to her surroundings and maybe meet up with some of the people she was to work with, but as soon as they arrived in the department, a nurse beckoned Dr Lombard over to one of the treatment bays.

'There's a little boy in here, a five-year-old, who's eaten a death apple, we think.' She frowned. 'He's in a bad way. Will you come and take a look at him? His name's Tyrell Dacosta.'

'Of course I will, Amanda. Poor little chap.' He turned to Jessie. 'Perhaps it'll help you get settled in if you shadow me for the next hour or so. The boss is busy with another patient or he would have greeted you himself. He asked me to look out for you.'

'Okay. That sounds like a good idea.' Jessie couldn't help feeling anxious about their small patient. She could only hope the fruit didn't live up to its awful name. It sounded ominous.

Hastily, she followed Robert and the nurse into the treatment room where a small boy lay wrapped in his mother's arms. He was whimpering and looked wretched, shaking and tearful, with a film of sweat on his brow and cheeks.

Dr Lombard introduced himself and Jessie, and then,

as he carefully examined the child, he asked the mother, 'So you think he's eaten a fruit of some sort that's upset him? Did he eat all of it, or just a little?'

'Most of it.' The young woman's face was pale and etched with worry. 'The tree was growing near the beach where we were walking. I spoke to my doctor on the phone and she said it sounded like manchineel. She told me to get him to drink a couple of glasses of milk and then to bring him straight here.'

She sniffed unhappily, close to tears, and Jessie could understand why she was so upset. There was some blistering in the boy's mouth and probably in his throat and stomach, too. 'Tyrell saw one of the apples lying on the ground,' the woman went on. 'It smelled good and he said it tasted sweet. I didn't know what it was so I told him to spit it out but I was too late, he'd already swallowed some of it.'

'Okay…' Robert acknowledged her sympathetically and then spoke to the little boy. 'Did the milk help take some of the pain away?'

Tyrell nodded warily, tears streaking his cheeks.

'That's good… Well, the first thing we'll do is get you a big white tablet to chew on. It will taste a bit chalky but it should help ease the pain even more. Can you do that for me?'

Again the boy nodded.

Jessie said quietly, 'This chewable tablet—is it a combination of antacid and proton pump inhibitor?'

Robert nodded. 'Yes, it's an anti-ulcer treatment. It should coat the damaged tissues and it'll help reduce the acid in his stomach.' He frowned and added under his breath, 'With this type of caustic ingestion there's always a danger that his throat might swell up, so we need to be aware of that in case he needs to be intubated. In the meantime, I'll give him an antihistamine injection.'

'Are you going to admit him?'

'Yes, I think we should keep an eye on him in case there are any complications.' He glanced at the nurse, adding, 'I don't want him to drink any water for a few hours—we need to let the medication do its work. Maybe a mild sedative will help. I'll write a prescription.'

A few minutes later, after making sure he had done everything he could to make Tyrell feel more comfortable, Robert glanced at Jessie and said, 'I have to go and put my notes on computer and deal with some paperwork in the office for a while. You might want to stay behind and talk to Mrs Dacosta and answer any questions she has. Do you think you'll be all right with that?'

Jessie nodded. 'Yes, that's okay. I can explain things to her if there's anything she doesn't understand.'

'Good. I'll come and find you as soon as I'm done.'

'Okay.'

Jessie talked to Tyrell and his mother, and after a while the nurse went away to take lab forms over to Pathology, leaving Jessie to try to put the woman's mind at rest.

Gradually, the little boy became drowsy. 'I think the medication's doing the trick,' Jessie commented quietly, keying in the settings for the intravenous fluid pump. The woman nodded, looking relieved.

A moment later, the door of the treatment room swished open and a man said quietly, 'Is everything all right in here?'

Jessie froze. Surely not… It couldn't be…could it? The softly accented voice came from behind her. It sounded horribly familiar, and she turned around in shock, only to have her worst fears confirmed.

Her breath caught in her chest. José Benitez was

framed in the doorway, looking impressively tall and
strong, clad in dark trousers and a crisp shirt with sleeves
folded back to the elbows to reveal well-muscled, tanned
forearms.

'Dr Benitez…' Her heart sank. How could this be happening? Why did he have to turn up here, of all places?
In fact, what *was* he doing here?

He inclined his head briefly in acknowledgement.
His eyes were dark and impenetrable. 'Dr Heywood—
Amanda told me I would find you here.' His gaze moved
over her, taking in her glossy chestnut hair, pinned back
with filigree clips, before flicking down over her slender
figure. 'How's our patient doing?'

Our patient. She scrambled her thoughts together. That
sounded as though he belonged here. 'He's a bit better, I
think.' She hoped the little boy was going to be all right,
but she was still worried about the possibility of complications and the matter of whether the fruit would live
up to its name of the death apple. She'd never heard of it
and she'd no idea of the devastation it could cause. 'His
pain level's gone right down and he seems to be comfortable for the moment.'

'I'm glad.' He picked up the boy's chart and scanned
it for a few seconds before hooking it over the bed rail
once more. 'It looks as though we've caught this in time,'
he murmured. He spoke to the boy's mother for a few
minutes, reassuring her about her son's condition, and
then said softly, 'Perhaps you'll excuse us, Mrs Dacosta.
I must speak to Dr Heywood for a while, but I promise
you the nurse will be back with you shortly.'

Jessie's heart made a heavy, staccato beat as she stood
up to leave the room with him. Her throat closed in a
spasm of disbelief. She'd had no idea he was a medical doctor—all this time she'd understood him to be a

marine biologist, concerned only with the conservation of the coral reefs in the area. How wrong that assumption had turned out to be.

He led the way to his office, which turned out to be a large, comfortably furnished room with a wide window that overlooked a pleasant landscaped area. Outside, palm trees stood out amongst giant ferns and flowering shrubs planted around a cobbled courtyard.

'Please, sit down,' he said, waving her over to an upholstered chair by the pale beech wood desk. 'May I get you a coffee?' It was merely a polite, formal offer, a way of observing the conventions of civility, but he was already standing by the sleek-looking machine, adding fresh grounds to the filter.

She managed to find her voice. 'Thank you,' she accepted, pulling in a quick breath and adding, 'I had no idea you worked here.'

'No,' he agreed. 'I gathered that. Actually, I'm in charge of the accident and emergency unit.'

She sucked in a breath. So he was her *boss*? Things were getting worse by the minute. 'You had the advantage over me,' she said, unable to stop a tinge of indignation from creeping into her voice. 'You must have known last night that I would be coming to work here today.'

'I guessed as much.' His eyes darkened. 'It was the one thing that reassured me we would be seeing one another again before too long. I didn't want to lose you so soon after meeting you.' He switched on the coffee machine. 'We needed a doctor to cover for our absent colleague, so I knew you must be her replacement. She's gone over to the mainland on extended leave due to unexpected family circumstances.'

'Yet you didn't think to mention this to me last night?'

He turned towards her and raised a dark brow. 'Perhaps I might have, but regrettably your brother came along and I think you'll agree things seemed to go downhill fairly soon after that.'

'Yes, unfortunately, they did.' She sent him a troubled glance. Was it really too late to sort this out? Perhaps she ought to try to put things right between them, not only for Ben's sake but because now it looked as though she would have to find some way to work with this man.

She said cautiously, 'I've had some time to think about my reaction last night and…perhaps I was a bit too hasty. Maybe I should have tried to see things from your point of view a little more. After all, it must have come as a huge shock to you to arrive home and find that strangers had invaded your house. You had every right to be angry, I do appreciate that, and I understand how you must have felt…but it really wasn't Ben's fault. You have to understand—I love my brother and I know him through and through. I know he can be a bit wild at times and he has his faults, but he told me he hadn't organised the party and I believe him.'

He made a faint smile. 'He's lucky to have a sister who is so ready to defend him. I hope he appreciates you.' He pressed a switch and steaming hot coffee spilled into porcelain mugs. 'Do you take your coffee white or black?' he asked.

'White, please.'

He used the steam wand to froth milk in a jug, topped up the coffees and then handed her a cup. 'Help yourself to sugar.'

'Thanks.' He'd listened to what she'd said, but he wasn't giving anything away. He probably still thought her brother was in the wrong.

She spooned golden sugar crystals into the coffee and

then sipped the hot brew carefully, unable to look him in the eye just then. She needed to gather her thoughts.

He was being polite to her, but that didn't mean he was prepared to forgive her for walking out on him last night. For all she knew, she could be out of a job by the end of the day. She wasn't used to being wrong-footed, but where this man was concerned it was beginning to look as though it might be something of a natural hazard.

Annoyed with herself for being so reticent, she put down her mug and sent him a wary glance. 'Am I going to lose this job because of what happened yesterday? I'd like to know where I stand.'

He studied her over the rim of his cup. 'Maybe we should start again and try to forget what went on between your brother and me. After all, as I said to you before, my quarrel is with him, not with you.'

She acknowledged his concession with a slight nod. It was way more than she might have expected and she was thankful for the reprieve, but inside she was still smarting over the unfairness of the situation.

'I was hoping you might have had second thoughts about keeping him on.'

'Not so far.' His tone was abrupt, his jaw clenching. 'Shall we agree to put that subject aside for now?'

She nodded reluctantly. What choice did she have? He was unrelenting in his attitude, and that was upsetting because she'd hoped to break through his tough exterior and appeal to his sensitivities. Perhaps he didn't have any where Ben was concerned.

At the same time, this job was important to her. It wasn't full-time but, even so, her salary had to pay for the rent of the apartment she was sharing with Ben—a place he'd had to find quickly after he'd been turned out of their father's house, and for the time being it would have to cover his expenses, too, until he managed to find some other work. 'I suppose we'd better,' she murmured.

'Good.' He frowned. 'What exactly were you expecting to get from working here?' he asked. 'Yesterday you mentioned you wanted to gain experience before you decide on a specialty—I can see that—but what else? Why here? Were you just hoping to spend some time with your brother and your father?'

He was quizzing her as though this was an interview, but she didn't see any point in being less than truthful. 'I was, of course…it means a lot to me to be close to them…but I also wanted to learn something about tropical medicine.'

'Yet you're planning to go back to the UK at some point, I expect?' He looked at her guardedly, as though her answer was important to him. This was only a three-month contract, but perhaps there was a chance it would be extended.

'Well, yes…but what I learn here will still be useful. With travel opportunities opening up all over the world, it's probably more important than ever to be able to diagnose unusual illnesses. And who knows, I might decide that I want to stay in the Caribbean.'

'That's true.' He seemed to relax and smiled properly for the first time that morning. 'I dare say you found yourself treading water in the deep end this morning,' he remarked. 'Did you have any idea what kind of poisoning you and Dr Lombard were treating?'

'None at all,' she answered. 'I'd never heard of the manchineel tree—it sounds as though it's very dangerous.'

'Oh, it is. That's why most of the trees are ringed with notices to warn people nowadays. Even touching the leaves can cause blistering, and if you're unwise enough to park your car near its branches during a rainstorm, you could find the paint stripped from it.'

She looked at him in astonishment. 'You're joking!'

He shook his head. 'I'm afraid not. In the past, the Caribs put their knowledge of the tree's features to good use. They found a way of dealing with their enemies by poisoning their water supply with leaves from the trees…and they used the sap from the branches to poison their arrows so that their victims would suffer a lingering death.'

Jessie shuddered. 'I'm glad we've managed to become a bit more civilised by now.'

He nodded. 'So am I. But it wasn't all bad. If any of the captives managed to escape they might survive if their tribe could treat them soon enough. They used to apply an arrowroot poultice to the wounds to draw out the poison.'

She made a face. 'I can see how the fruit earned its nickname—but thankfully it looks as though it's not always fatal. Tyrell will be all right, won't he?'

'Yes. He might have some discomfort for up to a couple of weeks, but I'm sure he'll be fine.'

José put down his cup and became businesslike once more. 'If you've finished your coffee, perhaps I should show you around the unit? It'll make things easier for you if you get acquainted with the layout of the place from the beginning.'

He laid a hand on her elbow, stirring up all kinds of warring sensations inside her as he gently steered her towards the door. She was all too conscious of his nearness, of his guiding fingers heating her skin. A tingling sensation ran in waves along the length of her arm, leaving her flustered and unsettled. There was no knowing why this man had such a potent effect on her, but after her experience back home, she had to steel herself against him. She couldn't risk letting herself be ensnared all over again. Besides, the man had sacked her brother. What on earth was wrong with her?

'You've already met Amanda and Robert,' José murmured, as they walked back into the treatment area. 'One or other of them will always be around if you need help with anything. I'm usually here, too, unless it's one of the days, like today, when I leave early to go and help out at the coral reef.'

She frowned. 'I had it all wrong from the beginning. When Ben mentioned his connection with you and the reef I thought that's what you did for a living—that you were a marine biologist or some such.'

He smiled. 'No, nothing like that. I see to the health of the divers and make sure everyone involved in the conservation work is okay. It's on a part-time basis, but I provide cover whenever I can. We actually need more people to fill in on occasion.'

'Oh, I see. Ben talks about the conservation sometimes. I know he enjoys helping out at the reef in his spare time.'

He nodded. 'He's a good diver and he's thorough in his research. It's just a pity he lets things slide in other ways.'

She frowned. 'He'll still be able to work with the group, won't he?'

'Yes, of course. I'm not in charge of the project.' His glance moved over her fleetingly. 'If you were interested, I could show some of the work we do. It would be good to have you come along with me.'

She wasn't sure how to react to his invitation. Would it be wise to get involved with him outside the hospital? Then again, maybe she could help sort things out for Ben by going along with him? 'Possibly.' She made a noncommittal shrug.

José didn't seem too concerned by her response. Perhaps he felt sure enough of her to bide his time.

By now they had reached the main A and E unit, and he showed her where equipment was stored and where she would find all the necessary forms. Theatre scrubs were kept in the locker rooms, but for the most part the doctors wore their own clothes when treating the children. 'It's less frightening for them,' he said.

Robert joined them a few minutes later as José was telling her about the daily routine in the department and their procedures for admitting patients.

'Hi.' He acknowledged José and gave Jessie a quick smile. He seemed preoccupied but said, 'I have to go and deal with an adult trauma emergency, so I thought you might like to look in on one of my younger patients— she's a three-year-old and has one of those tropical diseases we have to deal with out here every now and again. I don't know if you've heard of the chikungunya virus?'

Jessie thought about it. 'Isn't it spread by the Asian tiger mosquito? It can cause some nasty, flu-like symptoms and a lot of joint pain but, as I understand it, so far there's no cure.'

'You're right.' Robert's mouth curved. 'You've obviously been reading up on it.'

'Well, I thought I ought to do some research if I was going to come out here to work,' she said quietly. 'I hope there's something we can do for the child?'

'We'll give her supportive treatment,' José commented. There was a glimmer of satisfaction in his eyes. 'It's good that you've made an effort to get to grips with tropical medicine from the outset. Let's go and see how she's doing, shall we?'

'Okay.'

Robert hurried away to go in search of his trauma

patient while Jessie went with José to the paediatric treatment room, where a nurse was looking after the crying infant.

'Perhaps you'd like to take the lead on this one?' José suggested, and Jessie gave a cautious nod. This would be a testing time for her, and maybe he meant it to be that way. No matter that he was attracted to her, he was putting her through her paces to make sure he'd hired the right person for the job.

She'd heard of the virus, but she'd never treated anyone who had it, and certainly not a small child.

She spoke quietly to the child's mother and then attempted to examine the little girl, conscious all the while of José looking on. The toddler was obviously poorly, breathing fast, feverish and irritable, and it took a while to persuade her to let her check her over. Jessie looked at her eyes and mouth, felt her glands and listened to her chest with the stethoscope.

'She says her arms and legs hurt,' the mother said, 'even her hands…and she's burning up. Her brother has the same virus, but he's not ill like Marisha. She's really tired, and short of breath.'

'It can affect people in different ways,' Jessie explained, pushing her stethoscope down into the pocket of her cotton jacket, 'and Marisha does seem to have been unfortunate in her response. We can prescribe anti-inflammatory medication for the pain, though, and it should help to bring down her temperature.' She turned to the nurse. 'Would you set up an ECG, please? I'd like to see a printout of her heart rhythm.'

'Yes, of course.' The nurse quickly applied pads to Marisha's chest and started the trace while Jessie took advantage of the distraction to take blood samples from the little girl.

José studied the printout with Jessie. 'What's the verdict?' he asked in a low voice. He was assessing her, she was sure.

'Her heart rate is too fast—we need to slow that down and that in turn should help slow down her breathing. I suspect the virus has inflamed her heart muscle, causing congestion, so I want to prescribe a cardiac glycoside to regulate the heartbeat, along with a diuretic to control her blood pressure. And she'll need to have a low-sodium diet until she's managed to fight off the virus. She needs to rest and build her strength, so with luck she won't suffer any long-term effects.'

'*Excelente.*' José looked at her with renewed respect. 'I'll leave you to see to all that, then,' he said. 'She's obviously in good hands.' He started to walk away, but gave her a questioning glance. 'Perhaps we should meet up at lunchtime in the hospital restaurant and you can tell me how things have been going? About one o'clock?'

It sounded like more of a request than a suggestion, and she nodded, watching as he left the room a moment or two later. It seemed she'd passed the test…and relief flowed through her.

'How has the morning gone for you?' Robert asked when she ventured into the upper-storey restaurant a couple of hours later. It was a little before one o'clock. He stood alongside her in the queue at the food counter, loading his tray with a dish of curry and rice, and adding a dessert of passion fruit.

'Fairly well, on the whole, I think,' she told him with a smile. 'Amanda's been helping me out by showing me where equipment is stored, and so on. José showed me a fair amount, but there were bound to be gaps.'

They found a table by a window and Jessie was overwhelmed by the stunning view. Beyond the rolling, green-clad hills away from the town, she glimpsed the glorious deep blue of the sea.

José came to join them after a minute or two. 'I'm glad to see you're eating a hearty meal,' he said, looking with approval at Jessie's chicken ragout. 'You need to keep up your energy level in this job.'

He tucked into pork tenderloin with potatoes and root vegetables, listening as Robert and Jessie compared notes on the morning's work and interjecting occasionally to add a comment.

'How did you get on with our small patients?' Robert asked. 'I know you've had some experience in paediatrics.'

'Oh, the children are lovely,' she answered. 'Even the little girl who pushed a bead up her nose and didn't want to let me touch her.'

Robert chuckled. 'That's the only problem with treating youngsters—you need to get their cooperation or you're stymied.'

'I saw the girl who had the bead up her nose,' José said. 'I looked in on her as her mother was talking to the nurse. Her little brother pulled a pearl from the girl's hair ornament and tried to copy what she had done. I managed to stop him in the nick of time.'

They chuckled, and the conversation turned to the wonderful view of the harbour and coastline. 'Have you had a chance to explore any of the island yet?' Robert asked.

'Not really.' She shook her head. 'I stepped off the plane a couple of days ago and my brother showed me a beach nearby, but apart from that and a quick look around the area close by the apartment I haven't had much of a chance to do anything more. I can't wait, though. What

I've seen is so lovely. I'm really looking forward to visiting different parts of the island.'

'There's a small cove not far from here. Perhaps I could show it to you after we finish work here?' Robert suggested. 'Unless you've made other plans, of course?'

Jessie opened her mouth to answer, but José intervened smoothly, 'Actually, I was hoping Jessie might want to come along with me to the reef later this afternoon.' He sent her a quick glance. 'I thought you might be interested in the work I'm doing—you mentioned you might need to look for some other source of income to keep you going. This would perhaps be ideal for you.'

'Oh…yes, that's true, I did. I didn't realize…' So there was the chance of working at the reef? That hadn't occurred to her. She'd been too busy worrying about the pitfalls of spending time with José outside work to see that there might be an advantage in it. 'Perhaps…' She looked at Robert. 'I'd love to go to the cove with you some time,' she said awkwardly, 'but maybe I should take this opportunity to see if I would be able to do this? I could really do with the extra income it would bring in.'

'Of course. I understand. Don't worry about it,' Robert said. It was clear he was disappointed, but he put on a cheerful face. 'We'll do it some other time.'

José frowned and Jessie sent him a thoughtful look from under her lashes. Had he hoped to stop her from spending time with Robert? Perhaps he had an ulterior motive in getting her to go with him?

Well, maybe that wasn't such a bad thing. Wouldn't this be the perfect chance for her to plead Ben's case once more? After all, the man wasn't made of stone, was he?

'After work, then,' she murmured.

José smiled. *'Muy bien,'* he said.

CHAPTER THREE

LATER THAT SAME DAY, José turned his open-topped car onto the winding coast road, heading towards the harbour. It wasn't a long journey, but Jessie found herself loving every minute of it, watching the landscape change from the town with its pleasant market squares shaded by tamarind trees and palms, through forest-clad slopes and the gentle, undulating hills that led down to the clear blue waters of the marina. The sun was warm on her face and the soft breeze lifted her hair.

'Is it far to the reef?' she asked, after they'd reached their destination and he'd parked the car.

'Just a few minutes once we're on the boat,' he murmured. He lifted a case from the boot and they started to walk along the quayside. There were boats of all sizes in the yacht basin, their paintwork gleaming in the bright afternoon sunshine.

They followed a wooden mooring platform until José came to a halt by a large yacht, the *Bella Rosa*, white painted, with glittering steel guard rails all around the deck. Jessie stared at it. She was stunned.

'Is this yours?'

He nodded. 'I bought it about three years ago so that I could cruise around the islands and travel to the reef whenever I wanted. She's beautifully kitted out. I think you'll like her. I hope you do. Come on board and see what you think.' He opened up the deck gate and put out a hand to help her on board.

His grasp was strong and firm as he drew her along the ramp, keeping her close to him. He was long and lean, full of lithe energy, and as he helped her onto the deck, he was so near her that she could feel the warmth coming from his body. She felt the brush of his thigh against hers and her pulse quickened, heat rising in her. When he finally released her she felt almost disappointed.

She did her best to shake off those feelings. He was her boss and there was trouble between him and her brother—surely it was extremely unwise to be seduced into having such a strong awareness of him? She had to stop herself from being enticed into any kind of emotional attachment—she'd been hurt before, and who was to say José wouldn't turn out to be exactly the same kind of man?

Now, though, she looked around the yacht in open-mouthed wonder. Sun glinted on the polished, golden timbers of the deck, and glazed doors opened into a spacious salon that had been fitted out with sleek upholstered sofas and a low table. Wide, deep windows provided a panoramic view of the harbour.

Everything here was perfection, and she could imagine sitting here, taking in the air with an aperitif in hand. 'Wow,' she said, and couldn't resist smiling. 'Just…wow!'

He chuckled at her bemused expression. 'Let me show you around below deck.'

They went down into the galley, where pale oak exteriors housed a variety of equipment. 'There's a cooker, microwave, fridge and freezer,' he told her. 'Pretty much everything you might need.'

The boat housed two cabins as well as the master

suite, each one beautifully fitted out with the same pale oak that was the recurring theme throughout the boat. This was repeated in the main salon, where the wood-work gleamed faintly and luxurious fabrics added to the feeling of opulence. The room opened out into a dining area, and light poured in through windows all around.

'It's fantastic,' she said. 'I'm very impressed. I must say, this is a novel way to travel to work.'

He smiled. 'I guess it's the best there is.'

He took a bottle from the fridge in the galley before they went back on to the upper deck, and once there he produced a couple of long-stemmed glasses from a glazed unit in the cockpit.

'This isn't alcoholic, I'm afraid,' he murmured, pour-ing sparkling wine into the champagne flutes, 'as I have to pilot the boat and then be fit for work, but it's refresh-ing…and *you* can drink as much of it as you like.' He handed her a glass, then lifted his to hers with a gentle clink. His smoky gaze met hers over the rim. *'Salud!'*

'Salud!' she echoed in a quiet voice, and then began to waver under that intense, heated stare. She sipped her drink slowly, breaking off that eye contact.

He didn't say anything more but downed his wine and then, almost reluctantly, turned his attention to setting the boat in motion. She was relieved the moment had passed.

They sped across the water, heading towards a green outcrop some half a mile away, and after a few minutes José brought the boat to a halt at the dive site. Several men milled about on board another boat that was moored there. They were wearing wetsuits or shorts, and they were helping each other with equipment, compressed air tanks and masks and so on.

'Holà! Is everyone all right?' José called out, and they nodded. 'That's good. Permission to come aboard?'

'Aye, come on over.' The skipper grinned.

José retrieved his case and pulled out a large medical bag from one of the storage units on board, and then helped Jessie off the yacht and onto the dive boat. 'Let's hope the dive goes smoothly,' he said.

They stood on the open deck and watched as the men took to the water. 'What are they looking for down there?' Jessie asked. 'I mean, this is a conservation project—so what does that involve?'

'A few of the reefs in the Caribbean have been damaged over the years, for a number of reasons,' José explained. 'If the sea warms up too much because of climate changes, for instance, it can cause the coral to die off, or certain species of fish can cause problems by overfeeding. In time, algae and seaweed cover the reefs and block out the light.'

'Can something be done about that?'

He nodded. 'We reseed the reef with fast-growing coral species—we're having some success out here, and with luck we've managed to turn things around.'

He waved her to a chair on the deck by the guardrail. 'Please, sit down.' He took a seat next to her and opened the case he had brought with him, revealing a hamper full of mouth-watering food. 'I thought you might be getting hungry by now,' he said, 'so I stopped off at the restaurant and put together a hamper. Help yourself.' He handed her a plate and serviette, along with some cutlery.

'That was very thoughtful of you,' she said. It was totally unexpected, too, and she warmed to him even more. She'd been wondering when she might get to eat again. 'It looks delicious.' Her eyes widened at the variety of the contents—tortilla wraps filled with chicken, peppers, red onion and salad greens, along with potato salad and what turned out to be spicy corn bread. 'Mmm, this is good,' she murmured appreciatively, biting into a tortilla a moment later. 'I didn't realize I was quite so hungry.'

He opened a bottle of wine, filled a glass with the sparkling liquid and then passed it to her. 'There's coleslaw, as well,' he said, searching in the case and bringing out a container. 'And a tropical fruit salad for afterwards, as well as some fruit tarts.'

'You've thought of everything,' she said, smiling. 'This is wonderful.' She sent him an impish look. 'Is this how you spend *all* your working days out at the reef?'

He laughed. 'Not exactly. But today is rather different.' He looked her over, smiling. 'Today you are here.' The look he gave her made her insides tingle.

She blinked and swallowed hard. To bring things back on to an even keel, she asked quietly, 'So what does the work involve?'

He spooned black bean and rice salad onto his plate. 'I have to check the general health of the divers on a regular basis, and sort out any problems they might have. I need to keep up-to-date records, and I have to be here in case they get into difficulties. Mostly, the problems we see are to do with ear troubles and pressure injuries, as well as the occasional graze or scrape. These men are experienced divers, so on the whole they know how to avoid trouble. Even so, diving is a dangerous activity and we have to be constantly alert to things that might go wrong.'

She sipped her wine and looked out over the glittering blue water. A glint of silver caught her eye and she gave a small gasp of excitement as a flying fish leaped from the water and glided through the air on wing-like fins for a few moments before descending once more.

'That's one way to avoid being caught by underwater prey, I suppose,' José said with a smile.

'It's amazing, so sleek and graceful. I've never seen anything like that before.'

She peered into the clear water and was rewarded by the passing of a shoal of exotic, brightly coloured parrot-fish. She could see how they got their name—the external teeth formed what looked like a beak.

'Ben tells me about his dives sometimes,' she said, animated by everything around her. 'He says there are pinnacles down there, draped in seaweed, that look like trees and sway about in the water. And he showed me an underwater video he'd made of the reef, where you can see giant clams, sea anemones and sea fans—there was even a turtle trying to eat a sponge. It made it look as though diving down there is a wonderful experience.'

'It is. You could try a dive yourself one day, or maybe look at the reef by spending some time on a glass-bottomed boat.'

'Yes, I might do that.' She picked up an apricot-glazed fruit tart and bit into it, savouring the sweet taste on her tongue. 'Oh, I think I'm in heaven,' she murmured, closing her eyes briefly.

His mouth curved. 'An angel here on earth, definitely,' he said softly, letting his glance drift over her, and she blinked, looking at him guardedly, even as her stomach made a quick flip-over. She was flattered by his attention, and his seductive ways enticed her, calling out for a response that her treacherous body was all too willing to give…but at the back of her mind warning bells were ringing. She wasn't sure she was ready for any kind of flirtation. Perhaps she should be more careful in the way she acted around him.

He must have sensed her discomfort because he turned his attention back to the food for the moment and then said quietly, 'I wondered if we might see Ben here today. He often comes to the reef late in the afternoon.'

'Yes, I think he used to finish work at my father's distillery and come straight here—and then when he started working for you he carried on with the same routine.' She frowned and said with a hint of regret, 'But things are different now. He'll be out looking for work today.'

'Hmm.' José's eyes darkened. 'He does seem to have an unfortunate way of losing jobs. I know it upsets you, what happened between us, but I can't risk having someone unreliable on my team. Surely you can understand that?'

'Of course, but I hoped you would give him another chance. He's going through a difficult time right now, especially after what went on with my father.'

He broke off a piece of corn bread and dunked it into a small dish of salsa dip. 'He never really told me what happened between him and your father, only that there wasn't a place for him at the rum distillery any more.'

Jessie winced. 'They had a falling out. It was nothing to do with his work but more to do with their relationship. They've always had problems with one another ever since my father left when Ben was a small boy, but my father invited him to come over here recently and he jumped at the chance. He hoped that if he stayed with my father for a while they might get to know one another a bit better.'

'But things didn't work out?'

She shook her head. 'No, unfortunately not. They had a disastrous row and my dad told him to pack his bags and leave. He didn't even give him time to find somewhere else to live, so Ben had to stay with Zach overnight until he managed to sort something out.'

'That must have been a fairly spectacular disagreement.' He refilled her glass with sparkling wine.

'I suppose so…though, from what Dad told me, I think it all started over nothing, the way these things often do, and ended with Ben telling my father that his parenting skills were zero and he had no right to tell him what to do since he'd never been around for long enough to care about him—not a great deal since he was eleven, anyway.'

'Ouch!' José made a wry face. 'That must have stung.'

'Yes, I expect so. My father is very angry.' Her green eyes were troubled. 'But I think the main problem nowadays is that he married again, and his new young wife, his third wife, Hollie, doesn't see why we have to play much of a part in his life. She seems a nice enough person, but for some reason we haven't managed to get along as well as I would like. She probably feels that her security is threatened in some way.'

'It's possible. It's certainly a difficult situation for you and your brother…for your father, too, I imagine.' He studied her thoughtfully for a moment or two. 'Is that why you haven't gone to stay with him…because of the new wife?'

She nodded. 'Partly. I get the feeling she wouldn't want us there. It's as though we're intruding—which I suppose we are, in a way. The other reason is that I prefer to keep my independence.'

'So, what will you do now that this has happened?'

She shrugged lightly. 'I want to try to repair the relationship for all our sakes, with both my father and Hollie. I've been to see Dad and tried to talk things through, but it's difficult. Neither Ben nor I get on very well with our father after the way he treated Mum and walked out on all of us, but it's probably much worse for Ben. As a child he was confused and angry, and even now he finds it hard to come to terms with what happened. I think this

recent episode has upset him quite badly—it could be the
reason he started to drink too much and came to work
late. That's not the way my brother normally behaves.'

She wiped her hands on a serviette and looked out
to sea once more as a disturbance broke the surface of
the water. A figure broke through the waves close to the
boat and clung to the guardrail, pulling himself up. José
stood up and went over to help him at the same time as
the skipper appeared from within the cabin.

The man clambered on board and tugged off his diving mask. He was in his early twenties, Jessie guessed,
strong and muscular, but right now he was breathing hard
and his face was contorted with pain.

Jessie went to join José and the skipper to see if there
was anything she could do to help.

'It's my foot,' the man said in anguish. 'There was a
strong current down there and I slipped onto a sea urchin. It feels like my foot's on fire.'

'Okay, Tim, let's get you to a seat.' José and the skipper helped the young man to a chair, where José began
to inspect his injured foot.

'This looks nasty,' he said, and Jessie could see that
several spines or tentacles were embedded in the sole
and the side of Tim's foot. Some had broken off, leaving
black tips showing under the skin. 'I'll have to get these
out,' José said, 'because they can leave a poison in the
wound, and that's very painful.'

Already Tim's foot was red and swollen. José opened
his medical bag and drew out the equipment he needed—
a syringe, a vial of anaesthetic and tweezers.

'Would you like a painkiller?' he asked.

'Yes, if you have one.'

José handed him a couple of tablets and offered him
a juice drink to wash it down.

'Thanks, Doc. I appreciate it.' Tim managed a smile.

'Try to relax as best you can,' José told him. 'I need to inject the foot in several places, but the anaesthetic will numb it for you and then I can pull out the tentacles.'

Jessie rummaged in the medical bag until she found a kidney dish to hold the offending spines, and then she watched as José carefully dealt with each one.

'That's all of them,' he said finally, 'but there are still several tips lodged in there ready to cause trouble.' He looked closely at his patient. 'How are you doing?'

'I'm okay,' Tim said.

'Good. I think we'd best get you to soak the foot in hot water with some added vinegar.' He started to look in his medical bag once more, and triumphantly produced a bottle of vinegar. 'Always good to keep this to hand.'

Jessie said quickly, 'I'll go and get some hot water and see if I can find a bowl,' she said.

'Thanks.'

The skipper showed her to the galley, and she came back a minute or two later with a steaming bowl of water. 'It's hot, but hopefully not too hot,' she murmured.

José poured in the vinegar then tested the water. 'That's fine.' Glancing at Tim, he said, 'The heat should help to draw out the poison. You need to soak your foot for half an hour or so.'

Tim nodded and gingerly lowered his foot into the bowl. They all sat and talked for a few minutes, and as time went by Jessie was amazed to discover that the black tips were gradually starting to dissolve. 'That's incredible,' she said, watching the dots disappear to nothing. 'I really didn't expect to see that.'

'There is another way to remove them,' José pointed out. 'It may not be quite as effective, but if you brush the area with melted wax and let it cool, you can then carefully pull it away and it should bring the spines with it. But it's worth trying this first.'

He looked back at Tim. 'I'll write you out a prescription for more painkillers and some antibiotics,' he said. He started to put a temporary dressing on the foot. 'These things can become infected and we want to prevent that.'

Tim nodded and when José had finished he tried to stand up. 'I think I'll go to the cabin and get changed.'

'That's a good idea. It might be as well to rest for a while with the foot supported,' José suggested.

'Okay.' He nodded, and hobbled away with the help of the skipper.

José cleared up his equipment and then glanced at Jessie. 'What do you think about helping out here on a regular basis? Do you think it might suit you? I'll help you with the first few sessions, if you like, to ease you in gradually.'

'Thanks, yes, I'd love to take it on, and I'd be glad of the help in the beginning while I'm getting used to the different types of trauma.'

'Good. That's settled, then.' He glanced at the hamper. 'Would you like something more to eat or drink?'

She shook her head. 'I'm fine, thanks.'

'Okay. I'm sure the rest of the gang will enjoy finishing everything off.' His gaze moved over her. 'So, how has it been, your first day at work in the Caribbean? Was it what you expected?'

'Oh, it's not at all what I expected. It's been such an experience—the time just flew by, and then, coming here, I could never have imagined anything like this. It has been such a lovely end to the day, sitting out here on deck, watching the sun on the water and listening to the birds.' She smiled. 'I'm quite sure not every day will be the same.'

'I'm sure we could work around that, if it's what you wanted.'

He said it softly, his voice husky and seductive, and for a hot, heady moment she found herself wavering. Who could resist the temptation, the honeyed promise wrapped up in those words?

'Well, there's a thought,' she said on a shaky, slightly breathless note. 'That would be something to dream about, wouldn't it? A lovely, hopeless fantasy.'

CHAPTER FOUR

ON THE WHOLE, life in the Caribbean was turning out to be pretty good, Jessie decided. She spent her days working at the hospital, which could be hectic on occasion, like today, but in her free time she was able to explore the island with her brother or relax on a secluded beach.

It would have been idyllic if it weren't for her worries about Ben and her father, and for the conflicting feelings she had about her boss. It made her feel hot all over to imagine how easy it would be to succumb to José's subtle advances…but she couldn't risk it. How could she even think of getting up close and personal with the man who had turned his heart against her brother? Ben would never forgive her…and as for herself, how could she care for a man who was so unyielding, especially when he knew how much it hurt her? No, maybe the best thing to do would be to keep the relationship between her and José on a purely professional basis.

'Has your brother managed to find a job yet?' Robert asked, as they grabbed a moment to go through their patients' records together late one morning. He'd become a good friend to her over this past week, helping her to settle into the job, and she'd begun to confide in him a little. 'I know he was having a bit of difficulty finding anything suitable.'

She nodded. 'He's been set on by a company that makes furniture. They have him doing general labouring for now, but he'll gradually get to learn some carpentry skills.'

He sent her a sympathetic glance. 'It must be very different from what he was doing before. Your father was teaching him the distillery business, wasn't he? I suppose he was being groomed for some kind of management position?'

'That's right. That's how we understood it.' She gave a small sigh. 'It's been difficult for him, falling out with my father, coming to terms with losing that job and then being sacked by José. I feel so awful for him. He's beginning to think he's worthless, and no matter how much I tell him none of this is his fault he goes on blaming himself and trying to reason things out. Perhaps if José had given him a chance—'

'You still believe your brother is the innocent party?' Out of the blue, José's disbelieving, deep voice cut across the room.

Warily, Jessie turned and looked towards the door. He had come into the room without either of them hearing him, and now she stared at him awkwardly.

'You know I do,' she said flatly. 'He didn't take over your house for the party—that was down to Zach and Eric. And any problems he had in getting to work on time were because he was in a bad way mentally after my father rejected him all over again. It seems as though he's rejected him all his life. It's becoming a pattern.' She frowned. 'Perhaps if you'd found it in yourself to show him a bit of compassion and understanding, he would have been able to prove to you that he could pull himself together. As it is, what you did was like a kick in the teeth.'

'So I'm the one at fault here?' He sounded incredulous. 'Weren't you also rejected by your father?' His flinty gaze was obdurate. 'Yet I don't see you giving in to self-pity. No—instead you went to medical school and made a career for yourself.'

Her chin lifted. 'Ben is much younger than me. He was a child when my father left and he didn't understand what was happening. He needed his father. He was abandoned and he became disillusioned.'

'And because of that you mollycoddle him and make excuses for him when he makes a mess of things.' José's blue eyes lanced through her. 'You are a loving, caring sister, *chica*, but I'm afraid you are misguided.'

'And you are wrong,' she said firmly. 'You're hard and unbending, and I'm sorry that you can't see that.'

His dark brows rose. Perhaps no one had ever questioned his judgement before, but she wasn't going to back down now and she met his gaze without flinching.

She turned away from him, though, as the triage nurse hurried towards them, a worried look on her face.

'I need you to come with me right away,' Amanda said, looking at José. 'A couple of young girls have just been brought in. They've been suffering from dengue fever for the last few days, but one of them, Raeni, is showing signs of worsening illness. She's twelve. Her older sister, Shona, has been brought in because their doctor is worried she might go the same way.' She frowned. 'The parents are with the younger girl at the moment, but I'll suggest they sit with Shona while her sister is being treated. It might be too upsetting for them to go on seeing her like this.'

José stiffened, immediately on the alert. 'What are Raeni's symptoms?'

'The usual for dengue fever…bone pain, high temperature, vomiting and now a rash—tiny blood spots under her skin, and bruising. She's restless and her pulse is weak and rapid.'

Robert gave a low, concerned whistle. 'It's haemorrhagic,' he said under his breath. 'That's bad news. What about her sister? How does she compare?'

'She doesn't seem to be in such a bad way. She has muscle and joint pains, very bad headache, vomiting.'

'All right,' José said, already moving towards the door. His expression was deadly serious. 'Let's get them admitted to the observation ward. We'll do all the requisite tests, blood gases, serum, liver enzymes, platelets, chest X-ray…as you all know, this disease can be fatal, and we need to keep on top of it.' He shot Jessie a glance. 'You and I will work with Raeni. Robert and Amanda, I want you to take care of Shona. Let's go.'

Jessie had heard about dengue fever and knew how dangerous it could be if it became haemorrhagic. The patients would start to bleed internally and their organs might eventually shut down.

The problem for doctors was that the disease was viral in origin so only supportive measures could be put in place. There was no cure. Everything depended on the patient's ability to fight the illness and it seemed that children and the elderly were far more at risk than adults… and all this stemmed from the bite of an infected mosquito. It was very rare for this to happen, but when it did… She went cold with apprehension. Raeni was fighting for her life.

Pale-faced, she hurried over to the treatment room where the young girl tossed restlessly against her pillows. A film of sweat covered her body.

Jessie glanced at José. 'Shall I put in an intravenous line?'

José looked up from his examination of the child and nodded. 'Yes, please…Ringer's lactate. She needs fluids to replace the blood that she's lost and to keep her blood pressure from plummeting.'

He went on with the examination and said worriedly, 'I don't like the look of this bruising. If her condition deteriorates any further we'll have to give her a blood transfusion. Make sure we get a type match so we're prepared.'

'I will.' She would do everything to make sure this child had the best chance of recovery. She looked so fragile, so desperately ill.

Jessie worked quickly to set up the fluid line and then took blood from Raeni's arm for testing. 'I'll get these over to the lab,' she said, slipping the vials into their sample packets alongside the lab forms.

'Thanks.' José was preoccupied. He clearly cared very much about his young patient and was worried about her. 'Her fever's way too high and she must be in a lot of pain. Paracetamol should help, and it'll bring her temperature down. Maybe a sedative would be a good idea, too—the restlessness is probably a sign of insufficient tissue perfusion.'

Jessie nodded agreement. He was doing everything he could, giving the child oxygen through nasal cannulae, tubes inserted into the nostrils, rather than through a mask, which she guessed could be irritating for a child who was already stressed and feverish.

She hurried away to the lab and by the time she came back, José had everything under control. Raeni was hooked up to monitors that recorded her heart activity, blood pressure, respiration and oxygen levels, and if any of her vital signs dropped below an acceptable level an alarm would bleep.

'She looks calmer,' Jessie said in a low voice, 'and her temperature has dropped a little. That's good, isn't it?'

'Yes, but it might be deceptive.' His dark brows drew together. 'Things can change swiftly and there is usually a crisis point in these cases. The patient either gets better or...' His voice trailed away, but after a second or two he braced himself and gave her a searching glance. 'I can see you're worried about her, *querida*, but you need to be prepared for the worst. I know you care about all your patients...perhaps a little too much sometimes. I've seen how you follow the progress of your charges after they've been admitted to the wards.'

'I could say the same about you.'

He gave a faint smile. 'You could be right.' He added a few notes to Raeni's chart and then said, 'I do check up on my patients. I'd especially like to know what's happening with the three-year-old who was suffering from the chikungunya virus...Marisha? I've been looking in on her—there were complications and she developed myocarditis, but I haven't had a chance yet today to talk to the team looking after her.'

'She was so tiny, so vulnerable, I felt terrible, seeing her like that.' This was always the part of the job that hurt. Working with children could be rewarding, but it was also challenging and often stressful. 'I've been checking up on her, too—we've all been worried about her. The inflamed heart muscle caused her a lot of problems, but she's much stronger now and I think she'll be discharged tomorrow, as long as she rests at home and keeps to the low-sodium diet. Dr Morrison thinks she'll make a full recovery.'

'Good. I'm glad she's doing better. It's reasonable to send her home, provided we see her back here on a regular basis.'

'Mmm...I'll find out about that, but I'm sure it's all in hand.' She glanced down at the sleeping girl and then at the monitors. Her stats were not good.

'You should go and take your lunch break now,' José said. 'I'll stay with her.'

'Oh, no...it's all right. I can take my break later,' Jessie protested. She was concerned about this little girl, and every instinct told her to stay and look after her. 'I need to be here in case her condition starts to deteriorate.'

'No.' He shook his head. 'You've been on the go non-stop since early this morning and it's already well past your lunchtime. There are other doctors on duty who can help out. Go.' He made it a command, and she knew there was no point in arguing. He wouldn't change his mind.

Still uncertain, she reluctantly did as she was told, going to the locker room to retrieve her handbag and taking off the light cotton jacket she'd been wearing. She'd no idea that José had been aware of how busy she'd been up to now. But, then, he made a point of knowing everything that went on in the unit, so perhaps she oughtn't to have been surprised.

'Hi,' Robert said, meeting up with her as she left the emergency unit. 'Are you off to lunch? Do you mind if I join you?'

'I'd like that,' she said with a smile. 'How's Shona doing?'

'She's stable right now. We have her on a drip and she's been given painkillers, so she's comfortable for the moment.'

'That's good.' She walked with him along the corridor and glanced through the window that looked out over the hospital grounds. 'I thought I'd grab a pack of sandwiches from the cafeteria and then go outside and get some fresh air, if that's okay with you?'

'Sounds great.' He walked with her to the cafeteria, where they bought club sandwiches, chicken and bacon topped with salad, and cold drinks to wash them down.

'I could show you the beach nearby, if you haven't seen it already,' Robert suggested, and she nodded.

'I'd like that. I usually stay within the hospital grounds at lunchtime, so it will be good to go a bit further afield. How far is it?'

'It's only a five-minute walk. It's the cove I was telling you about...' He gave a wry smile. 'Before José decided we shouldn't get together.'

'Ah.' She thought back to that first day in the unit. 'Was that what he was doing? I wondered about that.'

'Well, he can't take his eyes off you, that's for sure.'

They left the hospital and walked along a couple of wide avenues until they came to a palm-fringed beach. Waves rolled gently onto white sand and rustic, thatched canopies were dotted here and there to provide shade from the hot sun. 'Shall we go and sit over there, a few feet away from the cabana? There's a bench we can use near the sea grape.' He pointed to a beautiful tree whose spreading branches bore long clusters of green grapes amongst its evergreen leaves.

'Good idea.' The timber-roofed cabana stood in the lee of the cliff, and the proprietor was smiling cheerily, selling all manner of goods that might enhance a tourist's stay on the beach. There were magazines and sunglasses, alongside an icebox of cold drinks.

They sat down and ate their food, watching the surf break on the shore. A small, yellow-bellied bird darted about, searching for nectar among the wild flowers that bloomed in crevices on the cliff side.

'I've noticed you've been quite reticent around José these last few days,' Robert said, tilting his head back to swallow the last of his drink. 'I think you're wise to be careful. Women fall for him all the time, you know, but he never gets serious with any of them.'

'He doesn't?' Her brother had hinted as much—something he'd heard from the people who renovated José's properties—but now Robert seemed to be confirming it.

'No.' He frowned. 'I don't want you to get the wrong idea—he's a brilliant doctor and a good man—but I can see he's interested in you and I know it would be easy for you to be tempted into responding, regardless of what went on between him and your brother. Somehow he has that effect on women—but I wouldn't want to see you get hurt, Jessie. Even in the short time I've known you I've grown to like you a lot.'

She gave him a wary smile. 'Thanks for that, Robert… thanks for the warning and for watching out for me. The fact is I'm not looking to get involved with anyone right now. I had a bad experience back home with my ex…and I guess I'm still licking my wounds.' She couldn't help feeling that if she were to get involved with José, the pain would be so much worse. Who was to say he would treat her any differently than he had treated any other woman?

'I'm sorry about that.' He gently squeezed her hand in sympathy. 'The man must be a fool to hurt you.' He looked around briefly at the sea lapping at the shore and up at the cloudless blue sky. 'But at least you came to the right place to try to get over him. Sooner or later, if you allow it, the Caribbean will heal your wounds.'

'I hope so,' she murmured.

Her stomach still clenched every time she thought about Lewis and the way he'd destroyed her trust. His actions made her question the wisdom of getting involved with anyone ever again. Wasn't he just like her father in being tempted by the grass on the other side of the fence? She was sad, thinking about her parents and their marriage. Her mother had loved her father dearly, with all her being, but he'd thrown that love away, choosing to go off with other women behind her back. It made Jessie feel sick to her stomach and it wasn't the kind of relationship she wanted for herself. Would José be any different? Were all men the same at heart?

They walked back to the hospital a few minutes later, and Jessie hurried to the room where Raeni was being treated. Robert went with her. 'I want to see how she's getting on,' he said.

José watched them come into the room together. His glance flicked over Jessie, moving from the shining chestnut waves of her hair, over the light-coloured sheath dress she wore, downwards to the soft, tan leather of her shoes. Oddly, he looked at Robert's feet, too, and then frowned.

Jessie was puzzled, but then as she followed the line of his gaze she realized what must be going through his mind. Sand crystals glittered in the welt of her shoes, and in Robert's, too. José must have guessed that they'd been to the beach together, and he didn't look at all pleased about it.

He made no comment, though, and Robert went off to take care of his own small patient. His mouth was set in a flat line and Jessie wondered if he'd picked up on José's dark mood or whether he was concerned about the wretched state of the little girl.

In the next minute, though, all these thoughts were banished from her mind as a number of alarms started bleeping. When she looked back at Raeni her chest tightened as she saw blood trickling from the girl's nose.

José gently checked inside Raeni's mouth. 'Her gums

are bleeding, too,' he said in a taut voice. He checked her hands. 'Her skin's cold and clammy. She's going into shock—she needs a blood transfusion, fast.'

They quickly set up the transfusion, and when they were finished José stood and watched over the little girl. *'Pobrecita. Espero que te mejores pronto.'*

Poor little thing. I hope you get well fast. Jessie knew enough Spanish by now to understand what he was saying, and it tore her apart to see the anguish flickering in the depths of his eyes.

He turned to her, his mouth set in a grim line. 'All we can do now is wait,' he said.

She nodded. He was always so much in control of things, but the strain was telling on him and she knew the plight of this child had rocked him to the core. 'I'll stay with her,' she said quietly, laying a hand gently on his shoulder. 'Perhaps you should go and find a change of scene for a while…maybe get a coffee or something to eat?'

'No.' He shook his head, reaching up to close his fingers lightly around hers. 'But thank you for the thought. I need to be here. There might be something more I can do to help her.'

'Then I'll bring coffee to you,' she said, gently disentangling herself. She would have liked to stay there, her hand in his, but someone might come along at any moment. 'I won't be long.'

She went to the staff lounge to prepare the drink, using the coffee machine that was housed in the small kitchenette. Amanda was already in there, taking her lunch break.

'I've just made a fresh brew,' the nurse said, adding milk to her own cup. 'The coffee here is wonderful—

José brings it in freshly ground from his grandfather's plantation. He won't drink any other kind.'

'I didn't know that—about the plantation, I mean,' Jessie said in surprise. 'I did think the coffee here was extra special, though—I guess I'm learning new things all the time.' She filled a cup with the hot liquid. 'Anyway, this is for José. He won't leave Raeni's bedside.'

'Ah. I saw how concerned he was. Has she taken a turn for the worse?' Amanda's brown eyes were troubled.

Jessie nodded. 'I'm afraid so. He's doing everything he can but he's very worried about her.'

'He's a wonderful doctor,' Amanda said. 'He's always been dedicated and he would do anything for his patients. He deserves the best.' She sighed. 'I know his private life raises a few eyebrows, because of his love-them-and-leave-them reputation, but I feel so bad for him sometimes. It's perhaps no wonder he behaves that way, after what happened with his girlfriend.'

'His girlfriend?' Jessie echoed, an unexpected stabbing sensation shooting through her stomach. 'What happened?' Her mind was racing. 'Was it something dreadful—was she ill?'

'Oh no, nothing like that.' Amanda's shoulder-length brown hair quivered as she shook her head. 'It's just that—but perhaps I shouldn't say any more. I've probably said too much already. I'm just repeating what was on the hospital grapevine.'

'I'd really like to know,' Jessie said, but Amanda wouldn't tell her any more, and frustration began to build up in her, tightening her stomach.

'Perhaps he'll tell you about it himself,' Amanda said. 'You could ask him. He doesn't talk about it very often, but we all knew that he thought the world of Rosa.'

Rosa. That name sounded familiar, but for a second or two Jessie couldn't quite place it. Then, with sudden chills running down her spine, she remembered...the *Bella Rosa.* That was the name painted on the side of José's yacht. Unaccountably, her heart sank and sadness washed through her. He loved the woman so much that he'd named his yacht after her.

Pulling herself together, she went back to Raeni's room a short time later and put the cup of coffee down on the bedside locker. 'How is she?' she asked, glancing at the girl and then back at José. He was carefully bathing the girl's forehead and throat with a cool, damp cloth. 'Is there any change in her condition?'

He shook his head. 'I'm afraid not. It's still touch and go.'

'I'm sorry. Do the parents know?'

'Not yet. I didn't want to worry them any more than necessary for now. If things change, I'll tell them.'

She sighed. 'Life can be so unfair sometimes.' She placed a pack of sandwiches on the top of the locker next to the coffee cup. 'I thought you might be hungry,' she said, 'so I brought you some sandwiches.'

'Thanks. I appreciate it.' He smiled at her, and her insides twisted painfully. There was so much she didn't know about this man, yet somehow, despite her reservations about him, she sensed they were two of a kind. He cared deeply about this young girl's well-being, that was clear enough, but underneath his professional exterior there were other deep emotions he wouldn't allow anyone to see.

It was beginning to seem as though she wasn't the only one who had suffered a betrayal. He, too, was bearing the scars, but this was altogether the wrong time to ask him about them.

The only difference between them, from what people had told her, was that he hid his pain by living his life with a reckless, devil-may-care attitude. He was surely heading for a fall.

CHAPTER FIVE

'Have you been here all night?' Jessie hurried into Raeni's room next morning and stopped in the doorway, stunned to see a weary-looking José sitting by the child's bedside. His dark hair was ruffled as though he'd been running his hands through it, and his usually pristine shirt was crumpled. His face was dark with overnight shadow, lending him a roguish air. Strangely, Jessie felt a compelling urge to go over to him and run her fingers through his hair. She wanted to hold him and let him rest his head against her chest.

Oblivious, he glanced at the gold watch on his wrist. 'Is that the time?' He blinked and stretched as though he was trying to force himself into wakefulness and then sent her a quizzical look from under his lashes. 'What are you doing here so early?'

She quickly pulled herself together. She shouldn't be having these thoughts about him. Her defences had been crumbling bit by bit and she needed to shore them up, fast, or she was heading for trouble.

'You wouldn't let me stay last night,' she said, 'so I had to come in as soon as I could this morning to see if she was any better. How is she?'

'She started to sleep peacefully about an hour ago.' He smiled and stretched some more, and Jessie's gaze was drawn to the muscles rippling beneath his shirtsleeves. 'The bleeding seems to have stopped and I think she's over the worst.'

'Oh, thank heaven.' Joy rippled through her. 'Her parents must be over the moon at the news.'

He shook his head. 'They don't know yet. Amanda showed them to the visitors' overnight room and persuaded them to try to get some sleep.'

'They'll know soon enough. They'll be so relieved.' She was so pleased she couldn't stop smiling, and José looked at her curiously, warmth creeping into his tired his eyes.

'It's good to see you smile.' He watched her for a moment or two, and then, with a small shake of his head, brought himself back to the matter in hand. 'Do you have any news of her sister?'

She nodded, her silky hair swishing lightly over her shoulders. 'I bumped into Robert on my way in here. He says she's doing okay.'

'Excelente.' He stood up and pressed the call button for a nurse to come to the room to keep an eye on Raeni. When she arrived a short time later he quickly updated her on the little girl's condition, adding, 'Stay with her and page me if there's any change for the worse.'

'Of course.'

'I should go and freshen up,' he told Jessie, his hand lightly cupping her arm. 'Come with me to my office and we'll go through the schedule for the day.'

'The schedule?' she echoed, as they left the room and walked along the corridor. She was finding it hard to think straight—the warmth of his touch sent little pulses of sensation to rocket along her arm at the same time as her heart began to thud heavily. It was thoroughly disconcerting and she had to force herself to concentrate on

what he had been saying. 'I assumed I would be working
with Robert in paediatric A and E as usual.'

'For some of the time perhaps, but I have to go out on
a call today and I thought it might be a good idea if you
were to come along with me. I've arranged for a doctor
to stand in for you in the emergency room. This way,
you'll get to see a bit more of the island, and perhaps it
will give us the chance to get to know one another better
and, who knows, make peace with one another?'

'Make peace?' She shot him a startled glance. 'I wasn't
aware we were at war. I thought we were getting along
all right.'

His eyes glinted. 'All right? Maybe. But underneath it
all we are at odds with one another—there's a vague discomfort between us, perhaps, an uneasy truce. Of course,
I do know that your feelings towards me are coloured by
my dealings with your brother, but I'm hoping we can
put that behind us.'

She sent him a sceptical glance. 'Do you really think
it will be that easy?' He let go of her arm as he pushed
open the door to his office and immediately she missed
that warm, intimate contact. Annoyed with herself for
her weakness, she said casually, 'Anyway, for myself, I'm
quite happy with the way things are at present.'

He gave a crooked smile. 'I guessed you might feel
that way. For *myself*, I think we are not truly *simpático*,
and I would very much like to change that.' He ushered
her inside the room.

'I do understand how you feel,' she murmured, 'but I
can't help thinking that what you have in mind might not
be very professional. You're my boss, and perhaps it's a
good thing we're not *simpático*. In fact, I think it's probably for the best if we keep a certain distance between us.'

To her surprise, he nodded. 'At work, yes—you are

quite right. That's how it should be. But outside work, we could get to know one another much better, don't you think?'

Much as she was inwardly drawn to the idea, she knew it could only bring about a whole host of complications. She shook her head. 'Not really... I think I'd prefer it if we leave things as they are.'

'*Eso no es bueno.*' He gave her a look of pained amusement. 'Why do you try so hard to resist me, *querida*?'

She studied him thoughtfully. 'Perhaps it's because I've heard about the kind of man you are. There's always gossip flying around, you know. People talk about how you never get too seriously involved with any woman. It seems you prefer to walk away before that happens. Perhaps I don't want to risk getting hurt.'

He sighed. 'I suppose there will always be talk. It's inevitable when you're in a position such as mine.' His eyes glinted. 'But you have no need to worry... I could get very serious about you, Jessie, if you were to give me the chance.' His blue eyes blazed warmly, inviting her to take up his offer.

Was it true? Would he really change the habits of a lifetime for her? It was unlikely, surely? 'It sounds as though your intentions are good, but how long would that last, I wonder?' she murmured. 'Have you ever stayed with a woman for long...long enough to really care about her?'

A muscle flicked briefly in his jaw. 'I have.' He was silent, and she guessed he didn't want to talk about it, but she persisted.

'What happened?'

'Things didn't work out.'

'Why not, José?' she prodded gently. 'What went wrong?'

'Things...fell apart.' He was struggling inwardly, she

could tell, fighting the urge to keep things hidden, but slowly, cautiously, he managed to get the words out. 'I don't think it was because of anything I did—or, at least, nothing I did specifically. I was with a girl for a couple of years—we were very close—' He broke off, his mouth making an odd shape. 'We even talked about getting engaged at one time.'

'But that didn't happen?' Jessie said quietly. Her throat was dry. She needed to know about his love life, but at the same time she wished it could stay hidden, something she didn't have to care about. It was becoming clear, though, that he must have had very deep feelings for Rosa, this woman from his past.

He shook his head. 'She changed her mind. And where I had once been thinking I'd found the right woman, the woman who could make me happy, she left me and went off with someone else.'

Jessie stared at him in shock. 'I'm so sorry. That must have been awful for you.'

He winced. 'It was a blow, I'll admit…to my pride as much as anything. And it was even worse when I found out that she'd married this man. I'd never understood till then what it felt like to be broken-hearted.'

She could sympathize with what he'd been going through. Hadn't she been hurt in much the same way? It was a pain that cut deep. 'Is that why you won't get too deeply involved with any other woman?'

'I suppose that might have something to do with it. Once bitten, as they say. It wasn't as though I was a raw young man when this happened, and I couldn't understand where things had gone wrong. I was bewildered for a long time. I didn't know why she'd had this sudden change of heart that made her want to leave me for someone else, and when I asked she couldn't tell me.'

'It didn't have to be anything you'd done, necessarily.' Her own father had behaved in just the same way, moving on when a more attractive proposition had come along. 'People can be fickle.'

'Yes. So I've discovered.'

Jessie exhaled slowly. Perhaps this explained a lot about why José would never get serious about any woman, as Robert had said. He didn't want to be hurt again, and that was totally understandable...but was he still hankering after the woman of his dreams?

'Do you see anything of her these days?'

'I hear from her occasionally, a postcard or a letter. She went to live on the mainland with her new husband and she lets me know how things are going from time to time.'

Jessie frowned. 'That must make things doubly difficult for you.'

He shrugged cautiously. 'I don't think about it. It's all in the past.' He looked around the office. 'We'll have coffee,' he said briskly, changing the subject and waving a hand towards the coffee machine. Clearly, he didn't want to talk about this any more. 'Have you eaten yet?'

'No, I'm afraid not. I left the apartment in too much of a hurry.'

'Nor me. I'm starving.' He smiled. 'There are croissants and strawberry preserve in the cupboard over there, if you want to help yourself. Oh, and you'll find a toaster with a warming rack on the shelf near the coffee maker.' He grimaced. 'I need to go and shower and change, but I promise I'll be back with you in two ticks. Make yourself comfortable.'

He went through a door into what must have been a shower room, because a few minutes later she thought she heard running water. That was unexpected, but perhaps it was a necessary facility if he stayed overnight from time to time, like last night, or maybe there would be occasions, after dealing with certain kinds of emergency, when he might want to clean up.

She set about heating up the croissants and made fresh coffee, all the while mulling over what he'd said. She certainly wasn't alone in feeling betrayed.

By the time she had finished eating her first melt-in-the-mouth buttery pastry, José had reappeared, looking startlingly renewed and refreshed, dressed in a fresh set of clothes. His black hair was damp from the shower, gleaming with iridescent lights, and his sheer vitality took her breath away. She stared at him, wide-eyed, drinking him in, bemused by her reaction to him. It didn't say much for her efforts to build up her defences, did it?

José poured himself a coffee and went to sit down opposite her by the beechwood desk.

Jessie took refuge in concentrating on mundane matters, asking him about his plans for the day. 'You said you had a call-out, but it doesn't seem like much of an emergency if we have time to stop for breakfast.' She slid a plate of croissants towards him. 'Not that I'm complaining—these are really good.'

He nodded. 'Amanda went out and fetched them for me. I usually bring them in fresh from the bakery every day…or sometimes, as a treat, my housekeeper makes the most delicious fruit tarts for me. Those are irresistible.' He kissed his fingertips in a gesture of remembered pleasure.

Jessie's mouth curved. 'It sounds as though you're very lucky to have her around.'

'It's true. I am. She comes to the house three or four days a week, to make sure my fridge is stocked and that I have fresh laundry and so on.' He cut a croissant in half and spread it with strawberry preserve. 'As to the call-out, I've been asked to take a look at one of the young workers on my grandfather's coffee plantation. He's been feeling unwell for some time, apparently, weeks or months, but kept shrugging it off. He said it was just a cold or some other virus. He insists he doesn't need time off work, but his mother is becoming concerned and my grandfather has finally persuaded the boy to let me take a look at him.'

She frowned. 'Wouldn't the boy's own local doctor have been the natural choice to give him a check-up?'

'Maybe. I don't know why the lad resisted for so long. But my grandfather wanted to help him and his family, so he turned to me…and I feel duty-bound to help out whenever he asks. I have a lot of respect for him.'

She could see from his expression, from the warmth that came into his eyes when he spoke about his grandfather, that he cared for him a good deal. 'Will I be meeting your grandfather?'

He shook his head. 'Not today, I'm afraid. He has to go and see one of his distributors in town.'

'Oh, I see.' She looked at him curiously. 'I was surprised to hear that your family owned a coffee plantation, but I'm looking forward to seeing it. It'll be a new experience for me. I don't know very much about coffee production.'

'I think you'll enjoy it. It isn't huge, but the Arabica coffee we grow is the best, the purest quality and it's sold in all of the coffee shops in the area, as well as further afield. It's very much sought after.'

He ate his croissants and then wiped his fingers on a serviette. Draining his coffee cup, he said with a smile, 'It was a long night, but I feel much better for that. Perhaps now we had better set off and try to find out what's troubling this young boy.'

'Okay.' She went with him to his car, and once again he drove with the top down, heading away from town, up into the mountainous interior of the island. The road took them through forests of mahogany and gum trees and leggy bamboo with their waxy, green leaves. Every now and again through the trees Jessie caught a glimpse of magnificent waterfalls cascading into winding rivers, and there were flowers everywhere, beautiful orchids and spiky scarlet heliconia. She drank it all in. It was awesome.

They reached the plantation in less than half an hour, and she stepped out of the car and stretched her legs. Everywhere was green, like an oasis.

A man came to greet them and immediately offered to show Jessie around. He was in his forties and his skin was bronzed by the sun.

'That won't be necessary, Simon,' José told him. 'I'll do that. But first I'd like to see Gabriel. Where will I find him?'

'I'll take you to him. He's working on the drying beds.'

They walked from the reception building through the plantation. The volcanic soil was rich and dark, Jessie noticed, and José pointed out the coffee bushes growing beneath the shade of broadleaved banana trees.

'The ripe coffee cherries were picked some time ago,' he explained, as they walked to an open area where coffee beans were spread out on racks in the sun. 'The cherries are passed through a machine that removes the outer shell and the pulp. Then they're washed and put into fermentation tanks for a couple of days to remove the rest of the outer layer. After that they need to be dried.'

Jessie looked around with interest. Workers, dressed

in light jackets and trousers and wearing hats to protect them from the sun's fierce rays, were raking the beans to turn them and expose every part of the bean to the hot sunshine. They all nodded and smiled as José approached. They recognised him and she guessed he must have been here lots of times. They seemed to be a contented workforce.

Sensing her interest, José went on with his account of what happened here. 'When they're dry they'll be milled to remove the husk, and then the green beans are put into sisal bags to be stored until an order comes in.'

Jessie frowned. 'They're not sent out straight away?'

He shook his head. 'As soon as an order comes in they're roasted and packaged ready to go. That way they stay as fresh as can be. That's the secret of good coffee—the freshness. The roasting, if it's done properly, brings out all the natural sugars, fats and starches—they're emulsified and caramelised and that's what makes the coffee special.'

'And the Arabica coffee you make here is extra special?'

'It certainly is.' He looked along the row of workers, his brows drawing together. 'I don't see Gabriel,' he said.

A young boy, about sixteen years old, was standing nearby, raking the beans, but now he stopped work to say, 'He was taken ill just a few minutes ago. He said he had a bad headache and then his nose started to bleed...he often gets nosebleeds, but this was the worst yet. We took him into the house so that he could rest for a while. Señora Benitez is looking after him.' He looked concerned, and Jessie guessed he was one of Gabriel's friends.

'You'll see that he's all right, won't you, Dr Benitez?' the boy asked. 'I think it's different this time. He looked bad…and he said there was something the matter with his eyes.'

José frowned, clearly worried about Gabriel's collapse. 'I will, Marco. Don't worry. I'll go and see him right now.'

The boy nodded. He obviously trusted José, and Jessie was touched by the rapport that seemed to exist between José and his grandfather's employees. Some of the older lads also appeared to be concerned about Gabriel's condition.

She went with José into the house, a white-painted wooden structure that had a veranda with comfy seats set out along its length so that people could relax and take in the fresh, warm air.

His grandmother came into the hall from another room when she heard José call her name. She was an attractive woman, with soft-looking silver-grey hair that settled into gentle waves, and when she saw her grandson her smile lit up her face.

'José, it's good to see you.'

'And you, Abuela.' José greeted her with a hug and a kiss and then turned to introduce Jessie.

'Welcome, Jessie,' Señora Benitez said. 'It's unfortunate that we meet when one of the boys is unwell—but I'm glad he'll be looked after by two good doctors. He looked so poorly and his nosebleed was really bad, but it's his eyesight I'm worried about.' She led the way upstairs to the guest room where Gabriel had been put to bed to rest.

She introduced them to Gabriel. 'José will look after you,' she told him. 'He's a good doctor.' Then she walked to the door and discreetly left them, saying, 'I'll go now. Let me know if you need anything at all.'

Gabriel couldn't be much more than sixteen years old,

Jessie decided. He was a good-looking boy, muscular from working out, she thought, but right now he looked in a bad way. He was propped up against snowy-white pillows and he was holding a blood-spattered tissue to his nose. There was a swelling above his cheekbone on one side of his face.

José went to the bedside and said, 'So, how are you, Gabriel? It looks as though you're in the wars.'

'My head hurts real bad,' the boy told him, 'and I kept having to blow my nose—it feels as though something's stuck up there. And now I can't see very well out of my right eye—I'm seeing double. *And* I'm going a bit deaf.' He looked especially disgruntled about that last malady. 'Mum thinks I don't hear her on purpose sometimes, but it's not true.'

José grinned in sympathy at that last vehement statement. 'Mothers can be like that sometimes.' He started to examine the teenager, looking at his eyes and checking his nose, mouth and lymph glands. 'You've been having problems for some time, haven't you...what is it, a few months?'

'Yeah. I thought it was a virus or something like that.' Gabriel looked searchingly at José. 'Is this a migraine? Is that why my head hurts and I can't see properly? My mother has those sorts of headaches.'

'I don't think it's a migraine,' José said, 'just a particularly severe headache. I can give you some painkillers for that, and I'll pack your nose with a dressing to stop the bleeding.' He studied the boy's facial features. 'How long have you had the swelling on your cheek?'

'Um...I noticed it a few days ago.' He shrugged. 'I suppose there's been something there for a while, but it's just got bigger lately.'

'Hmm.' José turned to Jessie. 'Perhaps Gabriel would

allow you to examine him—you could let me know whether you think it might be a migraine or a virus of some sort?'

Gabriel agreed to let her check him over, and when she shone a small light into his nasal cavity she thought she could make out a reddish-blue mass.

'Thanks, Gabriel,' she said when she had finished, and then she handed the small torch back to José. 'I don't believe it's either of the conditions you mentioned,' she told him. 'I think we need to get a CT scan to see precisely what we're dealing with.'

'Bueno. Mis pensamientos exactamente.'

His thoughts exactly. So she wasn't alone in thinking they needed to do some further exploration. If she was right in her possible diagnosis, Gabriel was suffering from an illness that mostly affected adolescent boys and could cause them considerable discomfort. At the moment, though, the teenager seemed to be more bothered by his headache than by the need to ask questions.

José handed the boy a couple of painkillers and poured juice from a jug on the bedside table into a glass so that he could wash them down. Then he set about packing the boy's nostril with gauze to put pressure on the blood vessels from within to stop the flow of blood.

'We could take you back with us to the hospital and get the scans done this afternoon,' he suggested when he had finished, 'if that's all right with you?'

'So soon?'

'We might as well. It'll save us another journey.'

Jessie knew José was deliberately making light of things.

'Would I have to stay in hospital?' Gabriel looked doubtful at the prospect.

'No, not today. But as soon as we have the scan results we'll be able to decide on a course of action. What do you think? Will you let us do that?'

'Okay. Will you talk to my mum?'

José smiled. 'Leave it with me. I expect she'll want to come with you. Anyway, in the meantime, why don't you lie back and rest for a while and let the tablets do their work?'

'Okay. Thanks.'

They left him and went downstairs to talk to José's grandmother for a while. 'I was so worried about the boy that I sent someone to fetch his mother, Amelie Torres,' she said. 'She was working in the packing room and she came right away. I took her into the sitting room and we've been having a cup of tea together. She called his father and told him what's happening—he was out making deliveries.' She looked anxiously at José. 'Is the boy going to be all right?'

'We hope so,' José said, keeping his answer purposely noncommittal. 'I'd like to talk to his mother for a few minutes, and then once his headache has eased off we'll take him with us to the hospital for tests.'

His grandmother winced. 'Poor boy. I think he tried to tell himself nothing was wrong, but we could all see he wasn't well. His mother's been despairing because he wouldn't see anyone about it, but I expect, like all boys, he just wanted to have fun and ignore anything that wasn't so good. I'm so glad you came out here to see him, José.'

He patted her shoulder. 'It's good that you were all looking out for him.'

A few minutes later, after talking to Gabriel's mother, Jessie and José went outside to wait for mother and son to appear.

'Your grandmother thinks the world of you,' Jessie

remarked quietly, as they wandered through the land-scaped gardens surrounding the house. Birds flitted through the trees, calling to one another or stopping to feed on insects or small fruits. 'It's very clear, from the way she talks and the way she looks at you.'

'I've always been close to my grandparents,' he said quietly. 'But sometimes it can be difficult to live up to their expectations of me.'

'What do you mean? I don't see how you could disappoint them in any way—you're a good doctor, a successful businessman, too, if all your properties are anything to go by, and you do what you can to help them out when they ask. How could you possibly *not* live up to their expectations?'

He made a wry face. 'I wasn't always a good grandson. I was reckless in my youth, and I suppose I must have caused them quite a bit of heartache. And, yes, medicine is a solid, well-thought-of career, but it's not what they wanted for me.' He gestured about him. 'Look around you,' he said. 'This plantation is their whole life, and they want someone to take over from them one day. They set their hopes on me, but it's not what I want. I knew early on what I wanted to do after I saw my cousin injured in a road accident. I made up my mind then that I wanted to be a doctor someday.'

'Ah…' She pulled in a quick breath. 'That is a problem… I can see how you must have been torn—and how they would want to keep this in the family.' She frowned. 'But what about your parents—wouldn't your father take up the reins?'

He shook his head. 'My father has never been interested in carrying on the family business. He's always been a free spirit, and goes wherever the fancy takes him.'

'And your mother?'

He looked sad. 'She was a wonderful woman…she died several years ago.'

'I didn't know—I'm sorry. It must have been a terrible loss for you.'

'Yes. I miss her—she was always loving, gentle and kind. I thought the world of her. I'd just qualified as a doctor when she died—it was a virus that affected her heart. I felt helpless, not being able to do anything to prevent the illness from taking her.' He frowned, looking at Jessie. 'But you lost your own mother—and quite recently too. Your feelings must be raw.'

She nodded. 'She was involved in an accident and suffered a fatal heart attack. It was a huge shock. Ben was only seventeen, so it was really hard on him.' She was lost in thought for a moment. 'We always want to turn to our mothers, don't we, especially in times of trouble, or even when we just want to share things with someone? I could always do that before my father left us. It was only afterwards that she became withdrawn.' She glanced at him. 'Were your parents close?'

'Oh, yes. They were very close. I was fortunate to be brought up in a house full of love…but after she died, my father lost heart. He decided he had to go away from here—there were too many memories to haunt him. He still travels a lot.'

'So you don't see much of him?'

He shrugged. 'A fair amount, actually. He comes home on a regular basis, and we keep in touch by phone or videophone.'

'I suppose those are good reasons why your grandfather has transferred his hopes to you. It must be difficult for you.'

He nodded. 'It is…because in the end I would hate to see all his work here go to strangers, and I don't like to disappoint him. Unfortunately, he doesn't think much of the way I live my life—the fact that I'm still unmarried and not settled with a brood of my own is another thing that bothers him, but there are some compromises I can't make, even for him. I'm not even sure any longer what love is. I thought I knew, but it turned out I was wrong.'

'I feel pretty much the same way. And, no, you can't go against your instincts to please your grandfather. In the end you have to do what's right for yourself.' Perhaps things might have been different if his ex-girlfriend had stayed with him. Having lost the woman he loved, how could he even think about settling down?

José's grandmother came out of the house, accompanied by Gabriel and his mother. 'They're ready to go now,' she said quietly. 'I know you'll take good care of them.'

'Of course I will, Abuela.' José hugged his grandmother once more and then helped Gabriel and his mother into his car.

'Are you feeling a bit better now?' Jessie asked Gabriel, when he was settled alongside his mother in the back seat.

'Yes, thank you. The headache is almost gone, and the nosebleed has stopped.'

'Good, I'm glad.'

She waved goodbye to Señora Benitez as José set the car in motion, and soon they were threading their way through the forest once more. Gabriel had recovered enough to look out of the window and comment on the scenery, even though he must be viewing it through one good eye, and Jessie smiled when he said, 'Look at that river—imagine diving from that bridge! It'd be fantastic!' In his boyish enthusiasm, he reminded her of Ben.

It wasn't long before they arrived back at the hospital,

and José showed the teenager and his mother into the waiting room. A short time later Gabriel's father came to join them. He looked distressed.

'Another nosebleed,' Mr Torres said, 'and now you can't see properly. We need to know what's going on, son.' He hugged the boy tightly, and seeing father and son locked in that warm embrace brought a lump to Jessie's throat. There was a lot of love there and she couldn't help comparing their circumstances to her own. When had her father last hugged her and shown her he cared?

'I'll go and organise the scans for you,' José told Gabriel. 'There might be a bit of a wait involved if the scanner's in use at the moment, but we'll fit you in as soon as possible.'

'Thanks. I think we'll be okay.' He gave his mother and father an uncertain look and they both nodded.

'Good. I'll come and fetch you when we're ready for you.'

Jessie followed him out of the room. 'I hope he's going to be all right,' she murmured as they walked over to the main desk. 'I didn't like the sound of his symptoms.'

'Neither did I.' José used the phone at the desk to set up an appointment with Radiology. Replacing the receiver, he said, 'They'll give me a call as soon as the scanner's free.'

'Good.' She sighed. 'Although I'm worried about what the scans will reveal.'

'That's understandable. He's a normal, energetic lad in every way and it's disturbing to see him like this. I've known him since he was knee-high.'

She nodded. 'I wondered about that—you've all been so good to him. It's wonderful to see how caring everyone is—his family, his friends, you and your grandparents. I just wish—'

She broke off. Some families could be intensely loving, and it made her sad that Ben's childhood had been so very different. Their mother had done what she could to make up for the wreckage of their family life, but Ben had been an impressionable boy and he had missed out on his father's love when he'd needed it most.

'Are you all right?'

José was looking at her, and she blinked away the tears that stung her eyelids.

'I'm fine. I just… I was just thinking how good it would be if Ben and I could have the same relationship with our father that Gabriel has with his. There is so much love there.'

'Hmm. Have you seen much of your father since you came out here—that *was* one of the reasons you came, wasn't it?'

'Yes, that's right. I've been to see him a few times. I wanted to talk to him about Ben, to see if I could help the two of them to make up, and I hoped that we might have some sort of father-daughter relationship.' She gave a broken laugh. 'He was always too busy when he was at home in England. I suppose he tried, but…' She drew in a quick breath. 'He's all we have left. Anyway, I went to see him a couple of days ago.' She bent her head, trying to hide her emotions from him.

'What happened? Did things go wrong?' He reached out and tilted her chin so that she had no choice but to look at him. 'Tell me, Jessie.'

'It was terrible. I was chattering on, talking about the apartment and saying how small it is and how things keep going wrong, like the roof leaks and the place needs rewiring.' She shot him a quick glance. 'Ben needed to find somewhere quickly after my father threw him out, and really we ought to look for a better place, but we're both busy people.'

She pressed her lips together. 'Anyway, my father's new wife was there—Hollie—and she seemed to think I was implying that he should pay for a new place for us. That never occurred to me…but she thinks we're after his money and that we want to undermine her.' She shook her head. 'It isn't true. All we want is to…' her voice faltered '…have our father acknowledge us…and…and be part of our lives. That's not too much to ask, is it?'

'Of course it isn't.' He wrapped his arms around her and drew her close so that her head rested against his chest. 'None of this is your fault. You're just trying to smooth things over and pave the way to some kind of relationship with your father. I'm sure he understands that.' He gently stroked her hair, trying to soothe her.

'No, I don't think he does.' She blinked, and tried to wipe away the dampness from her eyes. 'He says Hollie is his wife and he won't have her upset. She doesn't want either of us there and he told me not to visit again. I don't know what to do. I tried to make things better and now they're worse than ever.'

'Try not to worry, *querida*. Give him time and he'll realize that he needs you as much as you need him.'

'Do you think so?' She straightened and eased herself away from him a little. 'I don't know… He seemed so angry, so tense.'

'Perhaps inside he's fighting with himself. He doesn't know how to handle the situation.'

'Maybe you're right.' He was still holding her, and she wanted to stay like this, folded in his arms, secure and safe, but an inner voice was telling her that this could not be, she couldn't let this happen. 'I hope we'll work things out.'

She wiped her face with her hands and took a step back from him. 'I shouldn't have burdened you with all that. I'm sorry.'

'It's okay, Jessie. I'll always be here for you.' He frowned, looking at her closely. 'You know, if you need a decent place to live, I could help you find somewhere.' Then his mouth curved. 'I was going to say you could take a look at one of my renovated properties—but, better still, there will always be room for you in my own house.'

Hot colour flooded her cheeks. What exactly would he expect in return for that? 'Perhaps I'd give it some thought,' she murmured, 'but I doubt you'd want my brother to tag along, would you?'

He laughed softly and gave a light shrug. He might have answered, but his phone started to ring just then and he lifted the receiver to answer it.

'All right. Thanks for letting me know,' he said. Then he turned back to Jessie. 'The radiology team is ready for Gabriel.'

CHAPTER SIX

'So, you're saying I have a tumour?' Sitting in José's office with his parents an hour or so later, Gabriel stared at José in disbelief. 'But that can't be right.' He shook his head, his face ashen. 'You must have made a mistake. It's…it's a migraine or…or a virus.'

His parents looked traumatized, both of them in deep shock. Jessie sat to the side of the desk near José, wanting to help but staying quiet and letting José do the talking. The scans had shown everything clearly.

'I'm sorry, Gabriel.' José gave the boy a moment to absorb what he was saying.

'But I'm too young to have something like that, aren't I? How can it be happening to me?'

'What you have is a particular type of tumour that affects adolescent boys,' José said quietly. 'It's quite rare, but we think it has something to do with certain hormones that the body produces at this time. The thing to remember is that it's benign—that means it won't go to other parts of your body, and these kinds of tumours are usually slow growing.'

'And that's good—yes?' Gabriel looked doubtful, as well as shell-shocked, and Jessie's heart went out to him. He was struggling to take this in, and even though his parents were with him, ready to support him, essentially deep down inside he must be feeling as though he was all alone.

'It is. It also means we have time on our side so we can think carefully about how we need to treat it.'

'Okay.' Gabriel looked at him cautiously. 'Will I have to have an operation?'

'Yes. But we'll give you some tablets to take for a while to stop the tumour from growing, and hopefully to shrink it. It's a medication that counteracts the androgen responsible, and so it's not something that you can take long-term, unfortunately…but it should help your vision to clear once the pressure of the tumour lessens.'

He must have sensed that Gabriel was having trouble dealing with all this because he said, 'We can go over the treatment options at another time if you want. For now, perhaps you'd like to go home and talk things through with your parents?'

Gabriel looked relieved. 'Yes…yes, I'd like that.'

'Okay. I can give you some leaflets to read through if you want to take them with you. And, of course, if you have any problems or if there's anything you want to ask, you can get in touch with me at any time. I'll give you my number.'

José glanced at the teenager's parents. 'Were there any questions you wanted to ask?'

Mrs Torres gave a slight shake of her head. She looked stunned, unable to speak and close to tears. Her husband hesitated for a moment, looking uncertain, as though he wanted to speak but was finding it difficult to express himself. His features were strained, and it was obvious he, too, was having trouble coming to terms with what was happening to his son.

He said in a low voice, 'Will the medical insurance cover everything? We want him to have the best treatment, but…I'm not sure… Is there anything I need to say to the insurance company?'

'I don't want you to worry about that,' José said gently. 'My grandfather and I will liaise with the company for you to make sure everything goes smoothly. Gabriel will get whatever treatment he needs.'

'Thank you.' Mr Torres visibly relaxed as relief washed over him. 'Thank you so much for everything.'

'You're welcome.'

The three of them left a few minutes later, very subdued, walking slowly out to the car park where Mr Torres had left his car.

'It's a lot for them to take in,' Jessie said, going back into José's office after they had seen them off.

'Yes, it is.'

She looked at him thoughtfully. 'Insurance companies don't always cover every procedure in these cases—he'll need embolization, won't he, to seal the blood vessels in the area a day or so before the operation? There could be a risk of heavy bleeding otherwise, but from what I've heard that's not something all insurances cover.'

'Like I said, we'll make sure he gets the treatment he needs…and that includes embolzsation.'

So he, or he and his grandfather, or both of them, would pay the extra costs out of their own pockets if necessary. It said something of the bond that existed between his family and the people who worked for them and she looked at him with renewed respect. She smiled at him. 'That's more than generous.'

He shrugged lightly. 'We know the family—his parents have worked for us for years. They're good people and Gabriel deserves the best. He's a young boy starting out in life.'

His desk phone rang just then and he turned to answer it. 'Excuse me for a moment,' he said.

'Hola, Kiera, *que pasa?'* He mouthed to Jessie that it was his housekeeper on the other end of the phone.

Would you like me to leave? she gestured, pointing to the door, but he shook his head.

'Que puedo hacer por ti?' he queried, and then as his housekeeper answered he began to listen intently. Then, 'How could that be?' he asked. 'You're sure you've checked everywhere?' There was a silence, and he frowned, deep in thought. 'Okay, leave it with me. No, I'll see to it. Thanks for letting me know. *Hasta luego.'*

He replaced the receiver and was silent for a while, still thinking things through. His expression was sombre, as though he'd just received some disturbing news.

'Is something wrong?' Jessie ventured cautiously. 'Is there anything I can do to help?'

He shook his head. 'Nothing, I'm afraid.'

'It sounded as though you've had some bad news.' She wasn't sure why she was pushing the issue, but it bothered her to see him looking so troubled.

'Yes, I have.' He straightened up, bracing his shoulders, and then glanced at her. 'It appears that some things have gone missing from the house...valuable items.'

Her eyes widened. 'I'm so sorry. What was taken?'

'A couple of copper engravings—prints of a sea chart and a plantation house, together with the engraved copper plates that go along with the prints. They've been in the family for generations. They're seventeenth-century originals and unique. They've been valued at several hundred dollars.'

'It's no wonder you're concerned,' she said. 'Did somebody break in? Have they caused any damage?'

'No, there's no sign of that. In fact, no one's had

access since the night of the party because I had the locks changed.'

Jessie frowned, thinking about the implications of that. She sensed what was to come and when José spoke again he studied her searchingly, as though trying to gauge her response.

'They must have gone missing on the night of the party or in the time when the renovation work was going on. You do realize that has to mean your brother's in the frame for this, don't you?'

'Ben?' She shook her head, instantly denying it. 'No. Why should it have anything to do with my brother? Why is he the first to get the blame?'

A muscle flicked in his jaw. 'I think you already know the answer to that, Jessie. It's because he was there. He had the keys so he was ultimately responsible. He had access to the house before anyone else.'

'That still doesn't have to mean my brother was involved. Zach and Eric had access, too, as well as others doing the building work, and there were lots of people in the house on the night of the party. Anyone could have taken the prints.' She stared at him in shock. 'Anyway, why has this only come to light now? Perhaps you've simply misplaced the prints.'

He shook his head. 'They weren't misplaced.' He was adamant. 'They've been stolen.'

'So you say, but I can't believe this.' She didn't *want* to believe it and instead she was trying to work out what could possibly have gone wrong. 'They're probably in a cupboard somewhere. Perhaps they were put away while the renovations were going on.'

'I don't think so, but I'll check on that when I get home.'

She frowned, still unconvinced. 'Anyway, how would

anyone have managed to get them out of the house without someone noticing?'

'That's a good point,' he acknowledged with a slight nod, 'but they're quite small and would have fitted into a backpack quite easily. In fact, they were kept in the guest rooms, on display, so it would have been easy for someone to take them. Kiera only realized that they had gone when she went to clean the rooms today. The rooms haven't been used for a while, so there was no need for her to bother about them until now.'

Jessie frowned. 'I still don't see how you can accuse my brother of doing this. There must have been lots of people around at the time.'

'I'm not accusing him… I'm just saying, trying to warn you, that the police will be bound to question him.'

Jessie's face paled. Of course José would involve the police. She wanted to plead with him not to do that, but how could she when he was the injured party? But if he went ahead, what would that mean for Ben? He'd be arrested, questioned, perhaps even kept in a cell overnight, or longer, since he would be their prime suspect. And the apartment would be searched, all their belongings sifted through. How could he prove his innocence? Even if they didn't find the prints in his possession, they could say he'd sold them on. Things looked bad for him, really bad, and she didn't know what she could do to help him.

José was watching her closely. 'That worries you? Perhaps you're not so sure of his innocence after all?'

'That's not true.' Why couldn't he see that her faith was justified? Her chin lifted. 'I just think he'll be made a scapegoat, he'll be arrested and taken from his work and that will look bad for him and that might mean he'll lose another job—and then my father will have even more reason to find fault with him.'

He raised a dark brow. 'You don't think your father will see his side of things? That's unfortunate.' He sent her a penetrating glance. 'Has it never occurred to you that your father might have good reason to doubt him? You hear one side of it. Perhaps there's another.'

Her jaw tightened. Why was he so eager to take her father's side in this? 'I know my brother…a whole lot better than you do. And as for my father—' her expression and tone were cynical '—I'm not about to place much faith in what he has to say. Last time I spoke to him he seemed to think I had come over here to soak up the sun and go snorkelling with Ben and that I might occasionally take time out to put to put sticking plasters on a few cuts and grazes.' Her green eyes sparked dangerously. 'Maybe you think he has it about right?'

'No, Jessie, that's not what I meant. I just want you to look at this with a clear mind. I know you're upset—but you must see that I've been placed in a difficult position. How would you expect me to react?'

How could she answer that? He was perfectly right, perfectly reasonable in his thoughts and actions, but what she wanted was for him to hold her and tell her that everything would be all right, that she had no need to worry. But that was never going to happen, was it?

All at once it all became too much for her. She couldn't stay and listen to anything more. 'I'm sorry, I can't do this,' she said. 'I need to sort things out in my head.' Overwhelmed by the awfulness of the situation, she made for the door and swiftly left the room, heading for the changing room where she knew he wouldn't follow. Her emotions were fast running out of control and she needed to get herself together, to spend some time thinking things through.

When she had calmed down a little she took out her

mobile phone and called Ben. By now it was late afternoon and he would probably be about to finish work. Perhaps he could talk to his friends and find out if anyone
knew anything about the missing prints.

She could tell from his voice that he was appalled by
what she'd told him. 'I remember seeing them,' he said. 'I
had to move them when we were doing the renovations—
I was afraid they would fall or be damaged or at least be
covered in plaster dust—but I put them back when we'd
finished working on those rooms.' He sucked in a horrified breath. 'Does he really think I've taken them?'
She could almost see him shaking his head in disbelief.

'He thinks someone took them on the night of the
party, or just before that.'

'And I had the keys. I live nearer to the house than
any of the others, that's why he gave the keys to me, and
that's why the finger's pointed at me, first and foremost.'
His voice was taut. 'I'll ask around among my friends
and see what I can find out.'

'Okay, Ben. Let me know if you hear anything.'

'I will.'

He rang off, and Jessie stared into space for a few
minutes. Was there anything that she could do to put this
right? The whole thing was a nightmare.

By now her shift was over for the day and she col-
lected her bag and jacket and headed out through the
main doors of the hospital.

'Hey, Jessie,' Robert called after her, and she waited
while he hurried to catch up with her. 'Are you okay?'

'I'm fine.'

He gave her a doubtful look. 'Shall we walk along
together? I was going to head for the local market. It's
just five minutes from here. Do you want to take a

look around there before you go home? Unless you're in a hurry?'

'That's okay.' Maybe the distraction would help to take her mind off things and give her the space she needed to think clearly. She would come back for her car afterwards.

She glanced back at the hospital building as they walked towards the road and gave a small start as she saw José standing by the main entrance. He was frowning, his eyes narrowed, as he watched them leave. He must have come after her, wanting to talk to her, but he was too late. Right now, she didn't want to hear what he had to say.

Instead, she wandered around the colourful outdoor market with Robert, looking at the many stalls, bright with tourist souvenirs, beads, leather goods and clothes. She felt the warmth of the sun on her bare arms but it did nothing to cheer her.

They bought fruit and walked around eating seedless grapes as they listened to musicians tapping out a rhythm on steel drums in a cobbled courtyard, but for all this apparent relaxation Jessie still felt apprehension building up in her.

Robert picked up a leather belt and exchanged some light-hearted banter with the stall keeper while Jessie checked out the handmade crafts and bought a small beaded purse.

Eventually, after half an hour or so, they decided they'd seen enough for now and made their way back to the car park.

Standing with her by her car, Robert said goodbye, giving her a light kiss on the cheek. 'You've a bit more colour in your face now, at any rate.' He looked at her searchingly. 'I know there's something on your mind,

Jessie. I'm beginning to be able to read you. You don't have to tell me about it, if you don't want to, but are you going to be okay?'

'Yes, thanks. I'll be fine. I just want to get home.' She gave him a quick smile and after a few moments of hesitation he left.

Her phone rang as she slid into the driver's seat.

'Hi, Ben.' She spoke quickly, still keyed up by the news she'd heard earlier. 'Did you manage to find anything out?'

'No…at least not much. Only that Eric went to José's place today to pick up a cheque for some work he'd done and the housekeeper asked him if he knew anything about some things that had gone missing. My friend Sam was with him and apparently Eric said he knew nothing… but when they went back to the house they were working on he told Sam he'd seen me put something into my backpack that night.' She could feel his tension coming in waves. 'It was just the drawings for the building work, but no one believes me, Jessie. I'm going to get the blame for this because I was the one trusted with the keys.'

'But you didn't do it, Ben, and no one can prove otherwise.'

'Huh. Try telling that to Dad. He's already rung me, saying what's this about a robbery at the house where I was working? The news must have gone around like wildfire.'

Jessie frowned. 'But how would he have found out? José only learned about it himself this afternoon.'

'He said Hollie saw the housekeeper at the local store this afternoon and they were talking about it. He was questioning me as though he thought I was guilty— because I'd been out of a job and needed the money. He's my father and he thinks the worst. And that's exactly what the police are going to think, isn't it?'

'You can't be convicted of anything on hearsay.' It was worrying that people were talking about it already, and even more so that their stepmother was one of those who had found out. It would have been much better for Ben if their father had been kept in the dark about what was going on. As things stood, though, it seemed he'd already turned on Ben with his hurtful accusations. 'Try not to let it get you down,' she said soothingly. 'We both know you're innocent, and Dad will come to realize it, too, before long.'

'I can't see that happening. He was angry, Jess, saying there was no smoke without fire, and I threw it back at him and said if he hadn't put me out of a job and out of the house I wouldn't have been in that situation. Of course I didn't do it, but I was mad at him. He just proved he doesn't care about me at all.'

'I'm not so sure about that, Ben. The way I see it, you both said things in the heat of the moment, but when he's had time to calm down I think he'll come to regret his outburst.'

'I doubt that.' His tone was full of scepticism. 'He didn't regret throwing me out.'

'Well, maybe he did, maybe he was coming around to it, but then the robbery happened and set him off again. Give it time, Ben.'

'How can I?' She heard the despair in his voice. 'The police will come knocking at my door before they go to anyone else, won't they? And then I'll be left kicking my heels in a cell for a few days while they try to find evidence.'

'Look, I'll talk to José and see if anything can be done.' Right now she couldn't think what that might be, but she had to try, for Ben's sake. 'Just remember that you've done nothing wrong and have faith in yourself.'

He sighed heavily. 'I'll try.'

'Good. I'll see you later and we'll talk again. Try not to worry.'

'Yeah, it will be later... I'll be working overtime to-night.'

She cut the call and then sat for a minute or two, thinking about what she ought to do. Her heart was thumping heavily. She'd walked out on José—would he even be prepared to listen to her?

The Caribbean heat seemed to be sapping her strength, or perhaps she was simply too wound up and now she was running on adrenaline. She drove home and quickly showered and changed, letting the warm spray wash away some of her anxiety. As Ben was working overtime, she had the apartment to herself, and for once there was nothing to distract her thoughts.

If she was to talk to José, surely it had to be now and in person? It might already be too late, though... What if he had called the police after she'd left the hospital? How long would it be before they came knocking on her door? But she couldn't think about that now—she had to hope that he would at least hold off until he had been home to check the situation for himself.

She concentrated on making herself presentable, putting on a pencil-slim skirt and teaming it with a pretty camisole top. Then she added a light touch of make-up to her face and brushed her hair until it fell in silky waves over her shoulders. She checked her reflection in the mirror. That would have to do.

Driving along the coast road to José's house, she tried to work out what she would say to him. How would she plead her brother's case? What could she possibly say to make José change his mind? In his situation, wouldn't she want to get the police involved?

She parked at the front of his house and stepped out onto the paved driveway. The early evening heat descended on her as soon as she left the air-conditioning of the car behind.

She looked around. The house was every bit as beautiful as she remembered from the last time she had been here. Surrounded by shady trees and tall palms, it was a wide, two-storey building, white painted, with balconies encircling the upper floor and a veranda running around the whole of the ground floor. The white metal railings were moulded in a pleasing lattice design with gentle scrolls and swirls that were easy on the eye. There were flowers everywhere, along the borders of the driveway, with colourful shrubs set in gentle swathes around green velvet lawns.

She walked up to the porch and rang the doorbell and then knew a moment of panic. What if he was on the phone to the police already, or what if he didn't want to see her? What should she do?

The door opened. 'Jessie?' He looked at her, startled, his gaze moving swiftly over her. 'I wasn't expecting—' He broke off. 'Come in.'

'Thank you.'

He led the way into the lounge, a large, airy room with lots of tall, wide windows and glass doors leading onto the paved terrace where she had first met him. In here, the furniture was simple, with comfortable-looking sofas and a low coffee table, the wooden framework reflecting the white of the outside of the house, with soft touches of colour in the upholstery and in the sand-coloured floor tiles. Green ferns added coolness and depth to the room.

'This is lovely,' she told him, looking around and trying to absorb everything. 'I wasn't really able to take it all in last time I was here.'

He gave a wry grin. 'I dare say it was a bit difficult, with all the people milling around.'

'Uh…yes, that's true.' A flush of colour ran through her cheeks. Already she'd put her foot in it, reminding him of that night.

'I recall I promised you back then that I would give you a grand tour,' he said. 'We'll do that in a minute or two, if you like.' He gave her a look from under dark lashes, and she thought pensively how good-looking he was, how he had the ability to make any woman's heart flutter wildly. She was no exception. He was wearing casual chinos with an open-necked shirt that revealed the lightly tanned column of his throat. Already her pulse was thudding.

'Yes, that would be good.'

'Okay. But perhaps I could get you a drink first of all? What do you fancy?'

'Thanks. Anything that's cold and not alcoholic—I have to drive.'

'I think I have just the thing for you—how about orange and mango iced tea?'

'Okay. That sounds great.' He was being nice to her, polite and hospitable. How long would that last when he heard what she had come here to say?

She walked with him to the kitchen, a large, well-fitted room with a centre island and pale oak units finished off with smooth black granite worktops.

He went over to the fridge and brought out a jug of ready-prepared juice. 'I'll slice up some oranges to put in here,' he said. 'Do you want to grab a couple from the dish over there while I find a knife?'

She did as he asked, then waited while he carefully

sliced thin wedges of fruit and dropped them into the jug.
'Here you are,' he said after a while, handing her a tall
glass filled with juice and clinking with ice cubes. 'This
should help to cool you down.' He studied her once more.
'You look a bit flushed. Are you all right?'

'I…um…yes,' she murmured, taking a long gulp of
her drink. She decided to cut to the chase. 'I think perhaps I ought to tell you why I came here.'

'Hmm…I was wondering about that…though I'd be
glad to see you anytime without you needing a reason
to be here.' He smiled. 'It wouldn't be that you've given
some thought to my suggestion that you could stay here,
would it?' His blue eyes gleamed as he raised his tall
glass and sipped from it.

'Uh…no, actually, that wasn't quite it.' He was teasing
her, and she wasn't altogether sure how to respond. Even
thinking about spending the night under the same roof
as him was enough to knock her off balance. It wasn't
that she wasn't tempted…far from it… He had more than
enough charisma to coax her into his bed and she might
even dream about what it would be like to be with him…
but she'd been badly hurt before, and she wasn't looking to go that way again any time soon. Her experience
with Lewis had made her ultracautious. She didn't want
to go through all that heartache, the sickening feeling of
being let down, the abject misery of discovering the intimate betrayal.

She drank the remainder of her juice and put down her
glass. 'This is difficult for me,' she said, 'but…I wanted
to ask if you would hold off from calling the police. I
know I don't have any right to ask it, but my brother's in
a bad way emotionally right now, and I don't know how
he would cope if he were to be thrown into a cell for a
day or so. He didn't do anything wrong, I'm sure of it,

and I'm wondering if there's any other way we can find out what happened to your valuables and try to get them back?' She looked at him searchingly. 'I'm assuming you haven't already involved them.'

'No, I haven't, not yet.'

'Oh.' *Not yet*, he'd said. That meant he was still thinking about it. 'Then would you be prepared to consider holding off?'

He was silent for a moment and her hopes began to fade. Then he said carefully, 'I might. It's certainly something worth thinking about.' His gaze moved slowly over her, taking in the softly feminine curves outlined by the filmy material of her camisole top and the way the pencil-line skirt faithfully followed the smooth swell of her hips. His glance meshed with hers and colour began to rise in her cheeks.

'I'm pretty sure we'll be able to sort something out,' he said softly, placing his own glass down on the table. He smiled and held out his hand to her. 'If you've finished your drink, why don't we go upstairs?'

She drew in a sharp breath. 'I…uh…I beg your pardon?' Her eyes widened. What was he suggesting? Her heart started to pound, a heavy, fast beat against her rib cage, almost fit to burst.

'To look around the house,' he said, letting his hand fall to his side. 'I offered you a tour of the house and you accepted. I thought we could talk some more while I show you around.' He shot her a quick glance, his eyes glinting with mischief. 'I can see from your expression you thought I meant something else. Did you think I was propositioning you? Do you really think I'm the sort of man who would try that kind of thing?'

'Um…I wasn't sure,' she admitted.

He chuckled. 'Well, maybe I might, if I thought for a

minute you'd take me up on it,' he said candidly. 'But, you know, there could be another way we can get around the situation. We might be able to help each other out.'

'Really?' The tempo of her heartbeat had slipped into a rackety tattoo. No matter what he'd said, she knew, and he knew, that there was an age-old way of settling these kinds of dilemmas and there had been a whole wealth of meaning behind his invitation to go upstairs. But she hadn't taken him up on it, and now, in some wretchedly perverse way, she was wondering what it might have been like if she'd made a different decision. Why couldn't she give in to her primitive instincts and enjoy the taste of forbidden fruit, just this once?

She went hot all over at the thought. She must surely be the only woman who had ever thought about resisting him—what on earth was wrong with her?

'Come on.' He held out his hand to her once more, and this time when she accepted he led her out of the kitchen and up the wide, open staircase.

'There are two guest rooms along here,' he said, pushing open the door to each one in turn. 'The prints were framed on the wall by the wardrobe in each room. There's special glass to cover them and protect them from fading.'

The rooms were immaculately presented, with double divan beds in each and a wall-length dressing table and writing table combined along one side. In both rooms, a door led to an en-suite bathroom.

'The master bedroom is along here,' he said, taking her along the corridor. 'And there are a couple more family rooms. I chose this one for my own because it has the best view out over the sea. After the kitchen, it was the next room to be renovated. Come and take a look.'

She hadn't known what to expect, but the room was out of this world, something that she might only dream

of, with floor-to-ceiling windows on two sides, comple-
mented by floor-length drapes. The furniture in here was
sumptuous…a huge bed as the main feature, with luxu-
riously upholstered chairs at the other end of the room,
placed near a custom-made dressing table and writing
desk.

'There's a dressing room through there,' José said,
pointing out a beaded archway, 'and next to that there's
the en-suite bathroom.'

'I've never seen anything so perfect,' she said, looking
around in awe. He smiled, pleased by her response, and
slid his hand lightly around her waist, leading her across
the room towards the open glass doors and the balcony.

'You need to step out here,' he murmured, 'and take
in this view. I stand here every morning and tell myself
how lucky I am to be able to enjoy all this.'

She glanced at him. 'It isn't through luck, though, is
it?' she said softly. 'Surely, it has to be down to sheer
hard work? This hasn't all come to you overnight, has it?'

'I suppose not.' His mouth tilted in a wry grin. 'I studied hard for years to get my specialist qualifications, and
then when I was earning good money I invested as much
as I could in the property market. Things have turned
out well for me.'

The view from the balcony was breathtaking. From
this vantage point she could see the curve of the bay
where the blue waters of the Caribbean threw up foun-
tains of spray along the rocky shore. Closer to home,
the beach opened out into a wide stretch of golden sand
where palm trees swayed gently, their feathery green
fronds stark against an azure sky.

José kept his arm around her waist as they stood looking out at the beautiful vista, and Jessie did nothing to
discourage him. She liked the feel of his hand in the small

of her back, or where he let it come to rest on the rounded swell of her hip. She enjoyed the warmth of his touch.

'I meant what I said about offering you a place to stay,' he murmured. 'You could have one of the other rooms and look out at this view every day, if you wanted.'

Her mouth curved. 'That's very tempting—I really wish I could say yes. I'd like to stay here—I'd *really* like to stay—but you know I can't. For one thing, people would talk...'

'Does that matter?'

'It does to me. I don't want to be the subject of gossip. Besides, I know Ben needs me right now.'

'He's a grown man. He can stand on his own two feet—you just need to let him try.'

She shook her head. 'You don't understand how it is for us. When he emailed me in the UK it was a cry for help. I knew he was floundering, and he's still struggling now, though he's brash enough to try to cover it up. I couldn't leave him to fend for himself. He had to come to terms with losing a father, and then he lost our mother, too. He's doing the best he can, but he needs support for a bit longer, and I think that means having me close by.'

'He's very lucky to have a sister like you to watch out for him.' Slowly, gently, he turned her to face him, keeping his arms loosely around her. 'I just hope he deserves your faith in him.'

She looked up at him. 'Of course he does. I've never had any doubts about that.' Maybe if José was to invite Ben to stay as well, she might reconsider. In fact, she'd probably jump at the chance to stay here. Who wouldn't? But José didn't want her brother around, did he? That was a huge stumbling block, because Ben was family, and José would have to accept that she would always stand by him.

He was studying her closely. 'I think I'm actually jealous,' he murmured, his gaze trailing over her face, drinking in the contours of her cheekbones, following the line of her jaw, the slender column of her throat.

'Jealous?' she echoed. 'How can that be?'

His glance shifted to the pink fullness of her lips. 'I just wonder how it would be to have someone care about me that way, to have utter faith in me, and trust, and leave me with that overriding feeling of surety, to know that I was loved and wanted.' He shook his head as though to rid himself of the thought. 'Somehow I'm not sure that will ever happen.'

A breathy sigh hovered on her lips. Of course, he'd been in love once before, hadn't he? Only to have his world fall apart, as hers had done. A betrayal like that damaged people...she knew how that felt and she wondered at the strength of a man who could bare his vulnerability to her in that way. Against all the odds, she wanted to wrap her arms around him and help him find the comfort he was seeking.

Only he reached for her before she had time to even consider putting her thoughts into action. He bent his head and sought her lips, testing their softness with the brush of his mouth on hers.

The kiss was sweet and tender, a gentle exploration of all that she had to give, and as she responded with a shuddery sigh, he drew her closer to him, lightly pressing her soft, feminine contours up against the hard, muscled strength of his body.

Sensation upon sensation rocketed through her, and in those moments when he held her, she lost all sense of time and place. All she knew was that she loved the feel of his hands on her body, the way his palms stroked the

length of her spine, how he ran his hands over the planes
and hollows of her slender form.

'I've longed to do this since the first night we met,' he
said, his voice roughened, his breath warm against her
cheek. 'I wanted to kiss you and hold you in my arms—
you can't imagine how much I want you. When you went
off with Robert earlier today, it was like having a knife
twisted inside me.'

She was startled by the vehemence of his words. Did
he really resent her easy-going relationship with Robert?
'But we work together. We're friends.' Her head was still
in the clouds, her mind foggy with the glow of desire, but
a small thread of caution was starting to creep in on her.
'There's no reason why he and I shouldn't spend some
time together.'

'I know. I know it seems crazy and uncalled for. But
it's how I feel. I want you all to myself.' He kissed her
again, on the mouth, on her cheek, then shifted focus and
started to nuzzle the sensitive sweep of her neck, leaving a trail of kisses from the tip of her ear to the curve
of her shoulder.

She basked in a delicious, sensual haze, not wanting it
to stop, while her body tingled with exquisite pleasure…
But as the sun set over the horizon, casting a golden
glow over everything, reality was slowly starting to intrude, and she began to worry about the consequences
of her actions.

'José…I don't know about this…perhaps I was carried
away by the moment…but this can't happen. You're concerned about me being with Robert and so am I…about
getting into a relationship with anyone. We all have to
work together and it would be a mistake.'

'It's a little too late for that, now, *querida*, don't you
think? You and I are already involved. You couldn't hide

your response from me—I know that you want me as much as I want you.'

'But I shouldn't have let it happen and it can't go any further.' She looked at him, her green eyes troubled. 'I've been hurt before, José, and I don't want to face that again. I'm not ready for it.'

'You think I would hurt you?' His eyes darkened, became sombre.

'Not intentionally…but that's the way of things, isn't it? I need time to get my feelings sorted out.'

He eased himself back from her a little, his hands lightly circling her arms. 'If this man hurt you, he is worthless, not worth thinking about.'

'Even so…I need to get him out of my system.'

His eyes darkened. 'What better way to do that than with another man—with me? I can make you forget him, I promise.'

She gave a wry smile. 'That's probably true, but I don't want to take the risk.'

'Not even to help your brother? Not even if it was just make-believe?'

She drew in a shaky breath, throwing him an uncertain look. 'What do you mean?'

'It would help me a lot if you would think about playing the part of my girlfriend for a while. My grandfather complains that he isn't getting any younger and worries that I won't settle down. I think it's tiring for him, the arguments we have about this, and I don't want to cause him any more pain.' His blue eyes were troubled. 'He's already upset with me because I don't want to take over the running of the plantation, and I want to appease him in some way if I can. I'm very fond of my grandfather and I'd like to do something to make things better between us. If he thought I had a girlfriend he approved of, he might worry a bit less.'

'How do you know he'll approve of me?'

His mouth curved. 'How could he not approve of you? Besides, my grandmother thinks fondly of you already.'

'She does?' Jessie frowned. 'But we only met for a short time.'

'That's probably all it takes sometimes. She was impressed by the way you helped with Gabriel, talking to him and reassuring him, and she enjoyed meeting you.'

'Oh, I see.' She frowned. 'But surely she knows that you and I are not involved other than professionally?'

He shook his head, smiling. 'She told me she thought we were good together. She's a romantic, through and through, and I think she's already matchmaking in her head.'

He gently stroked her arms. 'So what do you think? Will you play along and make believe you are my girlfriend when I'm with my grandparents? And in return, I promise I won't ring the police about the theft?'

'So my brother will be safe—for now at least?' She sent him a doubtful look. 'Does this mean you're prepared to give up on finding the engravings? I can't see you doing that. After all, you told me how much they mean to you…to your family.'

He made a face. 'It may not come to that. Of course I'll do my best to find them. I'll check with sales agents in the region and ask them to look out for the prints. There's a chance I might get them back that way if they haven't already been sold on.'

He sent her a quick, searching look. 'You want your brother to be safe—but if by any chance he's involved, it's possible he'll still be found out when the prints turn up—you do realize that, don't you?'

She nodded. 'But he didn't have anything to do with it, so I don't have any worries there, do I?'

Except that if the prints turned up, they would have Ben's fingerprints all over them, wouldn't they? He'd told her he'd handled them, so that alone might incriminate him.

José's deep voice cut into her thoughts. 'As long as you're aware of the possibility.' He was still watching her closely, as though he was trying to capture her reaction.

She tilted her head back. 'You won't even consider the idea that he might be innocent, will you?'

'How can I know?' He gave a negligent shrug. 'I hope he is, for your sake, *querida*. But all that really matters to me is that you and I are *simpático*. What I can say to you is that if it turns out that he had anything to do with this, I won't prosecute him. Do we have a deal?'

She thought about it and then nodded slowly. What choice did she have? 'It's a deal,' she said.

CHAPTER SEVEN

'I WISH YOU didn't have to do this, Jessie.' Ben was troubled, impatiently pacing the floor of the apartment. 'Why should you have to act as his girlfriend? Let's face it, I didn't do anything wrong, so I don't see why you have to go along with this trickery. It isn't fair.'

'Fairness doesn't come into it. It was either that or José was going to call the police—I explained all that to you. I'm okay with this, Ben. You don't need to worry about me.' She swiftly checked her appearance in the mirror and then looked around for her handbag.

Ben frowned. 'I can't help it. I owe you so much already.'

She laid a reassuring hand on his arm. 'It's not going to be a problem, Ben.' She wasn't sure that was the absolute truth, but she didn't want her brother to worry. Inside, though, she felt a flutter of anxiety, strangely mixed in with a kind of pleasurable anticipation. José's kiss had stayed with her for a long time... Even now, she remembered the thrill of his encircling arms, the feel of his long body firmly pressed against hers and the gentle brush of his lips on her mouth and on her throat and bare shoulders.

A rush of heat ran through her body and she made an effort to pull herself together before the memories could lead her further astray. 'Anyway,' she murmured, 'I'm only going with him to the plantation today. It's not as though we're going to be alone. His grandfather's worried because there's some sort of problem with the crop, and José has to look in on a couple of the workers while he's over there. He thought it would be a good opportunity for me to meet his grandfather.' She glanced out of the window and saw José's car pulling up in the street outside the apartment. 'He's here,' she said. 'I should go.'

'Well, you take care, and don't let him push you into anything you don't want.'

'I will. It'll be fine.'

Sliding into the passenger seat beside José a minute or so later, she sent him a quick glance as he set the car in motion once more. He was immaculately dressed, in sand-coloured trousers and a crisp shirt that was open at the neck. His hands rested on the steering wheel, his skin lightly bronzed, with a smattering of dark hair along his forearms. There was a gleaming gold watch on his wrist. Just looking at him made her heart begin to thud and her body tingle.

'You said your grandfather phoned you this morning,' she said softly, trying to get things back on an even keel. 'He must be very concerned to ask you to go over there.' He nodded, his blue glance moving appreciatively over her before he returned his attention to the road ahead. Warm colour washed through her cheeks under that brief, but thorough, scrutiny. She was wearing blue jeans and a sleeveless top that flattered her curves, and her long hair fell in a silky curtain over her shoulders.

'There's some sort of blight affecting part of the crop. It could spell disaster for the plantation and the workers' jobs unless it can be stopped in its tracks.'

Her eyes widened at this bolt from the blue. 'I'm so

sorry. It must be tough, having to deal with something like that.'

'Yes, it's a blow. We need to figure something out, fast.'

His grandfather came out from the house to meet them as soon as José's car swept into the driveway in front of the plantation house. He was a tall man with vivid blue eyes and white hair that was neatly styled to frame his face. He wore beautifully tailored trousers teamed with a shirt and light jacket, giving him a dignified look that he carried off to perfection. He had the air of a man who was used to being in command.

'I'm glad you managed to get here so soon,' he said, greeting José by placing his hands about his shoulders and giving him a brief hug. 'I didn't know whether you would be at work.'

'Not this weekend,' José answered, smiling. 'It's good to see you, Abuelo.'

The old man nodded, turning to look with interest at Jessie, and José said quickly, 'This is our new doctor, Jessie Heywood. She's turning out to be a huge asset—we think a lot of her over at the hospital. She's very special.'

Señor Benitez raised a dark brow at that last comment, giving José a brief, thoughtful glance. Then he turned to Jessie, taking her hand in his and saying quietly, 'I am very pleased to meet you, Jessie. I have already heard something about you from *mi esposa*—just a little, you understand? You are welcome in my home.'

'Thank you. I'm glad José brought me along here to meet you.' She sent José a surreptitious glance. He had said she was special—had he done that purely for his grandfather's benefit?

José's eyes glimmered warmly as he returned her gaze. Maybe he knew what she was thinking?

To his grandfather, he said, 'Perhaps we should go and take a look at the plants that are causing all the trouble.'

The old gentleman's face became taut with anxiety. 'Yes. Come with me. I'll show you. They're in the northern quarter.'

They walked over there, following the paths laid out between the coffee plants, and once they reached the ailing section, José began to carefully inspect the leaves. Yellow rust patches marred the green and the new cherries that were beginning to form the second crop of the season were turning grey instead of vibrant red.

'Is there anything that can be done?' Jessie asked worriedly.

José frowned. 'We'll have to remove the worst of the crop and spray the rest up to a distance of around thirty metres away with fungicide.' He looked at his grandfather. 'I know you don't like to do that, but I don't think you have any real choice. Perhaps if you cut down some of the shade plants in this quarter and let the coffee bushes grow in full sun, they'll be less prone to this kind of disease. And, of course, we need to restock with resistant forms of the plant.'

Jessie looked at him with new respect. For all he said he didn't want to take much part in the running of the plantation, he seemed to know a lot about cultivation.

His grandfather looked on grimly. 'I was afraid you would say that. All these years I've stood out against using pesticides and anything other than organic ways of growing crops.'

José gave a faint shrug. 'I understand that, but in the end you'll have better yields if you fertilise with nitrogen and phosphorus. The plants will be healthy and less liable to be sickly. I don't see that you have any choice.

The damage isn't widespread and you could nip it in the bud. Why don't you try it, Abuelo?

The old man sighed. 'I suppose you're right. I'm set in my ways and perhaps it's time I moved on.' He sent Jose a hooded glance. 'Maybe you should think again about taking over. You're young and you have fresh ideas. That's what we need around here.'

José didn't rise to the bait. Instead, he smiled and said, 'You never give up, do you?'

'Why would I?' His grandfather's head went back. 'You are my grandson and I have high hopes of you—more than I have of your father, anyway.' He pressed his lips together. 'Let's go back to the house,' he said edgily. 'Your grandmother is baking cookies especially for you.'

'Okay.'

José slid an arm around Jessie's shoulders as they set off with Señor Benitez along the path that led back towards the house. All the time she was conscious of his grandfather's gaze resting on them as they walked along. José was making sure he knew that they were more than just work colleagues, and she had to admit that in her heart she wished that could be true. She wasn't sure quite how it had happened, but she was falling for him more and more each day.

Señor Benitez came to a halt when one of the field workers caught his attention, wanting to talk to him about something. 'Hi, Ramirez. What's the problem?' He turned briefly to José. 'You two go on, back to your grandmother,' he said. 'I'll catch up with you.'

José nodded, acknowledging Ramirez at the same time. 'All right, but I think we should go and see to our patients before we take time out to relax. I'm sure grandmother will understand. We won't be long.'

Señor Benitez inclined his head a fraction. 'I'll tell her.'

'Good. I want to see how Gabriel is getting along while we're here. Is he back at work?'

'Yes. He is…but you might want to look at Marco first. I sent him to lie down in the rest room. The lad hurt his back earlier today, lifting a sack of coffee beans. I've told him he should never twist and lift and that he should bend his knees when taking the weight, but you know these boys—they don't always listen.'

José gave a wry smile. 'I expect he'll do it the right way from now on.'

They moved away, leaving Señor Benitez to talk to the man, and José bent his head to Jessie's. 'I suspect,' he said in a low voice for her ears only, 'that this was all a ploy to get me over here so that he could work on me one more time. I'm sure he knows very well how to manage the plantation. He may look innocent, but he's a wily old man.' His hand came to rest lightly on the curve of her hip.

She nodded. 'I thought as much,' she answered softly, all too aware of the way his palm splayed out over the swell of her hip, and how he drew her close to his body as they walked along. 'But I can see he really loves this place and it's easy to understand how he would hate to let it fall into the hands of strangers.'

José's hand slid over her, squeezing gently. 'I know.'

His grandfather was still watching them as they walked away and she couldn't help wondering if this gentle caress was yet another attempt on José's part to show his grandfather that she was the new woman in his life. The thought saddened her…after all, she could get used to the feel of his arms around her and she didn't want it to be snatched away. He made her feel safe, cherished, as though she belonged by his side. Perhaps that was what she wanted most of all.

He looked at her. 'Are you okay?'

'Yes, of course.' She tried to shake off those wayward thoughts. 'I like him. I feel for him, that's all.'

'Believe me, I would never do anything to hurt him, Jessie. I want to put his mind at rest in any way I can, but I can't put my career in medicine on hold to look after the plantation. You understand that, don't you?'

'Yes, of course. It just makes me sad for him, that's all.'

He smiled. 'I think you'll find he's much stronger than you think. Now, shall we go and see Marco?'

'That sounds like a good idea,' she said.

He took her hand in his and led her towards a brick-built outhouse with white stuccoed walls. 'This is our first-aid centre,' he said. 'There's always a nurse on call here.'

They went inside and saw Marco, lying on a bed, supported by pillows. He was grimacing in pain as he tried to move.

José greeted the nurse warmly and then approached the bedside. 'Hi, there,' he said, looking at the boy. 'You've done yourself an injury, I hear. Do you want to try to stand up and show me where it hurts?'

The teenager nodded, and with the help of the nurse and José, managed to stand and straighten up. 'It's in my lower back.'

'Okay, let's see what's wrong.' José felt carefully along Marco's spine until he reached the trigger point.

'Ah...that's it,' Marco said, gritting his teeth. 'That's the exact spot.'

'Hmm. The area around your sacroiliac joint is inflamed,' José murmured. 'You'll need some anti-inflammatory medication to sort that out—it should relieve the pain and help to take the swelling down.' He glanced at the nurse, who was standing opposite them. 'I believe we have some diclofenac in the dispensary?'

She nodded. 'We do.'

'Okay, then.' He turned back to Marco. 'You can take a tablet right now with some milk—they're best taken with food and milk will do fine. It might help as well if you do some gentle stretching exercises when the tablets take effect. The nurse will explain them to you, and I'll give you a leaflet to take home.'

'Thanks, Doctor.'

'You're welcome. Take a couple of weeks off to rest up and get your back sorted...and remember to be careful how you lift things from now on. If something's too heavy, get someone else to help.'

'I will.'

'Good.' José smiled at him. 'Sit and rest for a bit while we find someone to run you home.'

Watching the interaction between them, Jessie realized that this plantation and its workers were more than a mere business enterprise. No wonder Señor Benitez was so attached to it. It was like a family venture—everyone knew everyone else and they cared about each other. And even though José wasn't here all the time, he must have visited on a regular basis because he knew everyone by name. She'd seen that for herself several times when he acknowledged people they came across. It made her warm to him even more.

José spoke to Marco and the nurse for a while longer, and then glanced at Jessie. 'I think we're done here for now. Shall we go and find Gabriel?'

She smiled at him. 'Yes. I'd like to see how he's doing.'

'You'll find him working over by the drying racks,' Marco said. 'He looks better than he did.'

'That's good. I'm glad to hear it. Thanks.'

They left the first-aid centre and went in search of Gabriel. As Marco had said, he was raking the coffee cherries so that they would dry in the sun.

José drew the boy aside to a quiet place where they could sit and talk. 'How are you feeling?' he asked him.

'I'm okay, I guess.' The sixteen-year-old was guarded in his answers. 'It feels weird knowing you've got something bad inside you that wants to keep on growing… It's a bit scary, you know?' He looked at Jessie and she nodded.

'I know. It's a lot for you to deal with.'

'But the tablets are helping?' José asked. 'The swelling seems to have gone down a bit.'

'Yeah. And I can see a bit better now.'

'I'm glad. We'll get you booked in for surgery.'

Gabriel nodded. 'I'll be glad to get it over with.'

'Of course. That's understandable.'

They said goodbye a while later, and Gabriel went back to his friends, leaving Jessie alone with José. They walked away from the drying area and headed towards the plantation house.

'I thought we might grab some time for ourselves before we go inside the house,' José said. 'You haven't seen the gardens yet, have you?'

She shook her head. 'No, I haven't, but it's all beautiful around here. Everything's so rich and green, like nature at its best—apart from the bit we saw earlier, of course.' She smiled. 'This is a busy place, everyone has a job to do, but it seems so peaceful.'

'It is, I know what you mean.' He led her to a secluded spot beyond the house. 'I want to show you the arbour—I think you'll like it.' He took her hand in his and drew her towards a cool-looking walled garden. A wrought-iron gate opened up to reveal a glorious display of shrubs and trees. There was bright colour everywhere, and Jessie's gaze picked out blue morning glory, snowy white gardenia and scarlet bougainvillea.

'It's lovely.' A delicate fragrance filled the air and she breathed it in deeply. 'This must be a favourite spot.'

'You're right. I often come here when I'm looking for peace and quiet. It's a very calming place. I sit on the bench over there and think things through.'

'Just like you do when you're out on your balcony at home.' They walked towards the rattan seat. 'You're very lucky...you know that, don't you?'

'I do.' They sat down by a jasmine-covered arbour, and José moved in close and wrapped his arms around her. 'I'm glad you like it here. It's good to see you smile.'

'How could I not appreciate it? Everything about the Caribbean has been a revelation to me. I'm loving every minute of it.' Along with every moment she was in his arms. She couldn't think now why she had spent such a long time trying to avoid the inevitable.

'I want you to be happy,' he said huskily. 'If you won't move in with me, at least let me help sort out your problems at the apartment. I could speak to your landlord, persuade him that he needs to abide by the building regulations, and my team could fix the leaking roof and any other things that need attention.'

'You would do that for me?' She looked at him uncertainly.

'Of course, like a shot. There's nothing I wouldn't do for you.'

She gazed up at him. 'You're very thoughtful... I've watched you, seen how you are with people—you're good and kind with everyone, not just with me.'

'But more especially with you, I think.' He smiled. 'You bring out the best in me. I meant what I said when I told my grandfather you are special…' He hesitated, then added softly, *'Pienso que me estoy enamorado.'*

Jessie looked at him, her eyes growing wide with wonder, but he met her gaze steadily, and she floundered. Did he mean what he'd said? He thought he was falling in love with her? Her heart began to pound.

'How could I not fall for you?' he said. 'You're beautiful, thoughtful, warm-hearted—everything I could ever want in a woman.' He bent towards her and kissed her gently on the mouth. 'Mmm…and heavenly kisses, too. You're my own sweet angel.'

He kissed her again, their bodies meshed in perfect symmetry, his lithe, muscled frame crushing the softness of her curves in a way that made every part of her respond with exhilarating, tumultuous delight. She wanted him, desperately craved his kisses, loved the feel of his hand moving slowly, possessively over the length of her spine.

'This feels so good,' she said in a ragged voice. 'How is it you can make me feel this way? I've never felt this way before.' She moved her body against him, urged on by the gentle pressure of that hand in the small of her back, a desperate yearning growing inside her. She wound her arms around his neck, let her fingers trace the line of his shoulders, feel the taut strength of his biceps.

'I've wanted to do this for so long,' he murmured, his voice thickened as he rained soft kisses over the silky column of her throat. 'I dream about holding you, kissing you, making you mine. I can't make sense of what's happening to me. All I know is I want to keep you near me. I don't know how I'm going to cope with being away from you.'

Her fingers stilled, coming to rest on the velvet-covered hardness of his rib cage. 'What do you mean? Are you saying you're planning on going away?'

He placed one last kiss on her soft, full mouth, then reluctantly eased back from her a little, his eyes dark, still smoky with desire. 'I'm afraid so. I have to go to Florida.'

'Florida?' She looked up at him, searching his face with troubled green eyes. 'When?'

'A couple of days.' He rested his head lightly against her temple. 'I should have told you before this, I know. I've been involved in the building of a new hospital wing over there—it's in the final stages of construction and I have to go over there and sort out the final details.'

She frowned. It had come as a shock to her. She'd been so used to having him around and she didn't know how she would feel if he went away. She would miss him. 'How long will you be gone?'

'A couple of weeks... I have to be back in time for my grandfather's seventy-fifth birthday party.' He smiled as he drank in her features, the oval of her face, the sweet, full curve of her lips. 'We'll go there together.' He pulled a face. 'It'll seem like an eternity, being away from you.' As though compelled, he kissed her again, a flurry of kisses trailed down over her lips, her cheek, her neck.

Two weeks...not too long, maybe, but long enough for her to feel desolate without him. She kissed him in return, revelling in that closeness, basking in the new realisation that he wanted her, needed her and that he was in as much emotional turmoil as she was.

A bird disturbed them, flying from the branches of a nearby tree to come and perch on the vines that rambled over the arbour. He chirruped, calling out in singsong fashion, and Jessie looked around to see what had caught his attention. Over by the gateway she saw that Señor Benitez was heading towards the secluded garden.

'Your grandfather,' she said in an urgent whisper, and tried to straighten herself. 'He's coming through the gate.'

José kissed her again. 'That's good,' he murmured, nuzzling her ear. 'He likes you. He'll be pleased...maybe he'll think I'm doing the right thing at last.'

'Are you?' she whispered. Or was she just one of a number in a long line of women who had fallen under his spell?

'I don't know,' he admitted huskily. 'I don't have any idea what I'm doing. For the first time in my life, everything's out of control. I feel as though I'm on a runaway train speeding along a track and I don't know where I'm heading.'

And wasn't she careering along a similar track—who could tell whether their journeys would come to a joyous end or whether they would fall headlong over the edge of a cliff?

'So there you are.' Señor Benitez looked from one to the other as though he was sizing up the situation, and then came to stand beside the bench. 'I've been looking for you.' He turned his attention to José. 'Your grandmother sent me—she has made some lunch, and we shouldn't keep her waiting.'

José stood up and held out a hand to help Jessie to her feet. 'You're right, we shouldn't,' he said. 'I just wanted to show Jessie the garden—it's one of my favourite places.'

And for Jessie it would be forever the place where she'd realized that she was falling in love...hopelessly, recklessly and chaotically in love with a man who didn't have any idea where he was heading.

CHAPTER EIGHT

JESSIE GLANCED AT BEN. 'I thought you were going out with your friends—shouldn't you be getting ready?'

'There's plenty of time yet.' He seemed preoccupied, and she guessed he was still worried about the prints that had gone missing from José's house. He'd been mulling things over for the past hour.

'If you say so.' Jessie put the finishing touches to her make-up and checked her image in the full-length mirror in the hall. 'Do I look all right?'

His glance swept over her. 'You look fine, Jess. You always look good.'

'I don't know—I've never worn this dress before. It might be a bit too casual for the party. José's grandparents are always smartly dressed.'

It was a simply styled frock with cap sleeves and a button-through bodice and a skirt that swirled around her legs as she walked. It was pretty, without being fussy, but it was sprigged with silver embroidery that added a touch of glamour. She cast another glance in the mirror and decided maybe it would do.

'They probably have to maintain standards in front of the workforce.' Ben frowned. 'You know, nothing's turned up at any of the auction rooms in all this time.

Whoever took the prints has either given up or must have sold them on in the first day or so.'

Jessie slipped her feet into a pair of high-heeled shoes and checked her watch. It was getting on for seven o'clock and José would be here any minute now. Butterflies were starting to flutter in her stomach.

'You could be right,' she said, 'but José seems to think that they're biding their time, waiting until the fuss dies down in the hope that no one will be checking up.'

'They would certainly have to know that they were worth something, otherwise why bother? But you shouldn't still have to pretend to be his girlfriend. How long will it go on for?'

She thought about that. 'I don't know. Until the culprit's found, I suppose.'

'You mean, until I've proved my innocence.' He gritted his teeth and then gave a heavy sigh. 'I'm sorry about this, Jess, really sorry I landed you in it.'

She frowned. 'No, don't feel that way. Anyway, it's all working out okay. It hasn't been what I expected.'

His eyes narrowed on her. 'You've fallen for him, haven't you?' He frowned. 'You need to be careful, Jessie. He has that effect on women, but his track record's bad. He doesn't stay with any of them.'

She tried to shrug off the suggestion. 'I like him,' she admitted, but even as she said it, she knew it was a wild understatement. Her feelings towards José were much more complicated than that. He'd been away these past couple of weeks in Florida to set up the new hospital wing and it had been a difficult, testing time for her.

'I missed him while he's been away.' She sighed. 'I suppose any pretence of being his girlfriend will all have to come to an end in a few weeks anyway, because my contract at the hospital finishes then.' All the time she'd been falling in love with José she'd forgotten that it could only ever be a temporary thing. 'I'll have to find something else or go back to the UK. I haven't made up my mind what I'm going to do.'

'Perhaps I should consider that, too,' Ben said. 'I'm not making any headway here with Dad. He doesn't seem to be very interested in seeing me.' He made a face and said in a disgruntled voice, 'I probably know more about José than I do about our father.'

'Do you really feel that way?' She was startled.

He nodded. 'I see José every time I go to the reef. He's always polite and friendly enough, considering what's gone on…but, then, you know how he is because you were there with him last time. I suppose he's a decent man, on the whole. At least he persuaded our landlord to fix the leaking roof and deal with all the other problems we were having.'

'That's true.' She smiled as she thought back to that time. 'I'm not quite sure how he managed it, but I imagine he knows people in the business.'

'Perhaps he shamed him into getting the repairs done. A lot of students stay in these apartments and they're supposed to be kept up to standard.' He sent her a quick sidelong glance. 'However he did it, it looks as though he put himself out especially for you.'

'I don't know about that. Maybe.' She tried to shrug off the suggestion, but it seemed Ben had already worked out that something was going on between her and José. Had he guessed that she had strong feelings for him—that she loved him?

'Anyway,' Ben said, cutting into her thoughts, 'how are you getting on with his grandparents? Do they really think you're his girlfriend?'

'I think so. I've been over to the plantation a couple

of times since and they seem to have accepted me. They haven't said an awful lot about us being together, so to speak, and José hasn't pushed anything too much. He knows I feel awkward about deceiving them and I don't want to let them down when we eventually stage a break-up. Not that we've talked about that yet.' She frowned. 'I like them both and I feel bad about upsetting them.'

José knocked on the door of the apartment a few minutes later, greeting her with a smile. He flicked a gleaming glance over her and nodded approval. *'Eres bella, querida,'* he said softly.

'Thank you.' He thought she was beautiful. She felt a glow of heat start up inside her. She'd missed him more than she might have imagined and now her heart was hammering and she couldn't think why he was having this effect on her.

Ben hovered in the background, watching them, and for a while afterwards both men regarded each other with a degree of caution.

'You need to take care of my sister,' Ben said in a warning tone. 'Make sure you treat her well.'

'Of course.' A gleam of respect flared in José's eyes. 'You can believe it.'

Jessie frowned. She didn't want to be the subject of discussion between the two men, and perhaps they caught that from her expression because nothing more was said. José and Ben locked glances and seemed somehow in those moments to reach some kind of understanding.

She left the apartment with José a short time later, sliding into the back seat of the waiting taxi.

'I heard that Gabriel came in for another scan the other day,' she said, as the cab driver took them along the main road out of town. 'Did you get a chance to look at the results?'

'I did. The tablets are definitely doing the trick.' The car wound its way towards the coast. 'The tumour has shrunk a little and the double vision has cleared up, so that's good news.'

She smiled. 'Yes, it is. Have you set a date for the operation?'

'He'll be operated on tomorrow. I've spoken to the surgeon and he did the embolization a couple of days ago. The surgery's complicated, as you know, but he's very skilled and I'm confident he's the right man for the job.'

'Let's hope so.' She hadn't expected the surgery to take place so soon, but at least it would be an end to Gabriel's anxious waiting.

They arrived at the harbour a few minutes later, and the driver dropped them off by the quayside.

'Where are we headed for?' Jessie asked, puzzled as José started to lead her along the jetty. 'I thought the party was going to be held at a hotel or a bar.'

'It's something a little grander than that—it's my grandfather's seventy-fifth birthday, after all. My grandmother decided he had to celebrate in style.'

They walked a little farther and her eyes widened as she caught sight of a yacht lit up in the distance. Even from there she could hear the beat of salsa music along with faint laughter of the guests on board.

'Whose boat is it?' she asked.

'My father's. He wasn't sure whether he'd be able to be here today, but he arranged everything.' His expression was momentarily serious. 'I wish my mother could have been here to celebrate with us—she would have loved the glitz and glamour.'

He helped Jessie on board and they were immediately greeted by a waiter carrying a tray of glasses filled with white wine. José took two glasses and handed one to her. *'Salud,'* he said, taking a sip, and she did the same.

'Salud.'

Jessie drank her wine and felt the warmth curl in her stomach. 'Mmm, that was good, and this is just the start of the evening.'

He smiled. 'It's from my father's wine cellar—nothing but the best for my grandfather. He loves him dearly, but he could never cope with restrictions. My father's a wanderer…or, as some say, a bit of a loose cannon.'

'Oh, dear. That doesn't sound good.'

'Well, it means he can't be trusted to take on the plantation. He prefers to design boats.'

She looked around. 'So this must be one that he worked on, I suppose?'

'Yes, he did.'

They finished their drinks and wandered into the main salon, where a group of musicians was entertaining the crowd.

José's grandmother came over to them. 'Ah, you're here,' she said, flinging her arms wide and giving José a hug. 'How long has it been—a fortnight?' she chided him. 'You need to come and see us more often.'

'I will, Abuela,' he said, looking contrite. 'But I had to go to Florida on business—the work is almost finished now, so I won't need to go there so often.'

'Ah…you should tell that to your grandfather. He misses you.'

'I'll talk to him.'

'He'll be pleased. He's been worrying about the roasting machine. Problems, problems. It's his birthday and still he worries.'

She turned to Jessie and took her hand in hers. 'It's good to see you, Jessie. You look lovely. Come and talk to my husband while I go and organise the birthday cake.' She turned to José. 'Will you come and help me? I was hoping you and I could wheel it in, rather than have the waiters do it. Then, when he's seen it and blown out the candles, I'll send it back to the galley to be cut up.'

'Okay.' He laid a hand lightly around Jessie's waist. 'I'll take you over to my grandfather.'

Señor Benitez was sitting comfortably on a couch at the far end of the salon, talking to friends, but they made room for Jessie and his grandson when they approached. José kept his arm around Jessie as they stood facing him.

'It's about time you turned up,' the old gentleman said, looking sternly at José. 'You leave me in the lurch when my machines start to play up. I'm getting on in life, you know. I can't do this for ever. You need to keep that in mind.'

José grinned. 'Happy birthday, Abuelo. I can see you're in fine fettle and you know very well you're fit for another couple of decades at least. Why didn't you call Nick to come and look at the machines? That's what you pay him for.'

His grandmother answered the question for him. 'Because he thought he could fix them himself.' She rolled her eyes heavenward. 'Anyway, come…let me take you away for a moment.' To Jessie she said, 'I promise I won't keep him for long.'

Señor Benitez patted the seat beside him and gestured Jessie to sit down. 'He needs stability,' he said, watching José walk away with his grandmother. 'Too much racketing around with women who are totally unsuitable, but it was to be expected, I suppose.'

Jessie flinched. Was he including her in his condemnation? She couldn't help wondering what else he was going to let out of the bag. 'Unsuitable?' she murmured. 'In what way?'

'They want his money or his status…or they're just out for a good time.' He made a dismissive gesture. 'These last few years he seems to have lost his way.' He fell into a brooding silence for a while, and Jessie began to feel uncomfortable. She was just about to say something to try to lift his mood when he said, 'He was completely off the rails as a boy—it was hardly any wonder, with no guidance from his father. It's an absolute miracle he's turned out as well as he has.'

Jessie relaxed a little. 'You do think he's made good, then?' she said with a smile.

'I do.' He studied her thoughtfully. 'I'm sure you'll help him to get back on track, though,' he said confidently, a faint smile hovering on his lips, and Jessie gave a small inward gasp.

The old man didn't appear to notice her discomfort. 'He needs to prepare to take over the plantation,' he said firmly. 'It's his birthright.'

'Shouldn't that belong to his father?' she asked on a tentative note.

'Pah! His father has no interest in it at all.' His bright blue eyes softened. 'But José is special. He's a good man. He will do the right thing, I am sure of it. He just needs a little push.'

A commotion disturbed them, and Jessie looked up to see José and his grandmother wheeling a trolley towards them, loaded with a huge tiered cake decorated with white roses and silver ribbons, and with candles aflame on top.

Everyone started to sing 'Happy Birthday' and Señor Benitez became misty-eyed. People crowded round him as he blew out the candles and Jessie moved to another part of the sofa to give them room.

'He's happy,' José said, looking at Jessie. 'Don't take too much notice of his crotchety manner. He's soft as butter underneath.'

'I was beginning to work that out.'

He smiled down at her, and leaned over to plant a kiss on her startled lips. 'I knew you and he would get on well. I saw you talking to one another. He was smiling—that's a good sign.'

He kissed her again, taking his time, easing himself down onto the seat beside her. His arms slid around her. 'My beautiful girl,' he murmured. 'I've missed you, and your lovely smile—and I've missed your lips. I need to taste them every day, feel their luscious softness.'

He bent to claim her mouth once more and she whispered quickly, 'People will see, José.' She pressed her palm against his chest in a futile effort to ward him off.

'That's the point, isn't it?' he said in a low voice, amusement darting in his eyes. 'We want my grandparents to see that we're together as a couple. That's probably the best present my *abuelo* could have. Kiss me, my sweet. Show me how much you care for me.'

He kissed her again and this time, no matter that her head told her this should not be happening, her body definitely had other ideas. Every nerve ending quivered, her body strained to meet his and her lips softened and parted in response to his kiss.

'Let's get out of here,' he said a moment later, easing back from her to look at her flushed face. His voice was roughened, 'We'll go on deck and get some air. We can dance out there, if you want.'

'All right.'

All at once, she wanted to be with him more than

anything. It was a beautiful star-filled night in the Caribbean, and the moonlight cast silvery beams over the water. The sky was a deep, cerulean blue. There was perfume in the air from the flowers on board the yacht. It was magical.

Trying to keep her defences intact suddenly seemed such a waste. Why shouldn't she give in to her instincts and go willingly into his arms?

The band was playing a haunting, romantic tune, and when José drew her towards him and wrapped her in his arms, they stayed together as one, swaying gently to the music, thinking only of each other. She laid her head against his chest and drifted with the music and he kissed her again, a gentle, shifting sigh of a kiss that made her senses swirl and filled her head with dreams of what might be.

How had it happened that she'd fallen in love with him? It was sheer madness, but she felt as though she was being swept away on a fast tide and she was powerless to do anything to stop it.

They danced and in between times helped themselves from the vast array of food that was being served on the aft deck. There were prawns and crayfish with spicy sauces, peppered beef, salads with smoked cheese and red onions, and a variety of desserts—raspberry tart, ginger-snap baskets with ice cream and fresh berries, and vanilla panna cotta.

The party was a huge success, and Señor Benitez and his wife had a wonderful time, judging by their smiling faces. As the night wore on, though, they pleaded tiredness and retired to one of the rooms below decks. Some of their friends would be spending the night on board, and in the morning they would go on with the celebrations.

'Shall we get out of here?' José suggested some time

later, holding Jessie close. 'There are too many people here and I want to be alone with you.'

'I think that's a great idea.' Her voice was husky, her mind hazy with wine and music and the sheer joy of being with him. 'Where are we going?'

'To my place? I wouldn't want to go back to your apartment and find Ben there.'

'Okay.' She was pensive for a moment or two, thinking back to the friction between him and her brother earlier. 'You shouldn't take anything he says the wrong way, you know. He's only looking out for me.'

He smiled. 'I know. Actually, I think he's all right. The more I get to know him, I don't believe he did anything wrong—how could he when he's inherited the same family genes as you?'

She stared at him, her mouth dropping open a little, the breath catching in her lungs. 'Do you mean it?'

'I do.' He took swift advantage of her parted lips, kissing her with such tender expertise that she felt her limbs go weak and every part of her being responded to him with pure desire and heady longing.

She didn't remember much of the drive home, except for being in his arms in the back of the taxi, lost in a wonderful world of new, joyous love. She'd never felt like this before, so utterly sure of herself, knowing that this was what she wanted, being with him. Nothing else mattered. No one had ever made her feel like this. Anything that had gone before was simply no comparison. All her doubts had been swept away with the touch of his lips on hers, with the feel of his hands gliding along the smooth line of hip and thigh. He was so much more worthy of her love than any man. There could never be anyone else.

He paid off the driver and let them into the house. "Let

me look at you,' he said, as soon as the door was closed. His gaze ran over her from head to toe. 'I can scarcely believe that I have you all to myself. You're gorgeous, Jessie. I could get lost in your smile.'

They hadn't even made it into the living room and she looked at him through a misty veil of love, a gentle smile tugging at her lips. She wanted him. Her green eyes must surely be giving out that message, loud and clear.

He gave a soft, ragged groan, pulling her towards him, and she let her clutch bag slide to the floor. 'Sweet girl,' he said softly, 'you're everything I've ever dreamed of.'

'Am I?' she murmured teasingly. 'Am I really?' She lifted her arms, clasping them loosely around his neck, running her fingers through the silk of his hair. She loved the feel of him, the strong column of his neck, the smooth skin of his shoulders, the firm muscles of his arms. She ran her hands over him, testing the velvet hardness of his chest beneath her fingertips.

In turn, he slid his hands over the bodice of her dress, deftly releasing the buttons and laying bare the white lace of her bra and exposing the creamy swell of her breasts above the half cups. The breath caught in his throat as he looked at her.

'You're so beautiful, Jessie…exquisite. You take my breath away.' He slid his hands inside the bodice of her dress, his fingers cupping her breasts.

He kissed her again, gently nuzzling the slender line of her throat, and she pulled in a shaky breath. Did she actually know what she was doing? Was she ready for this? Her body trembled with yearning. Wasn't it already too late?

'Let's go upstairs,' he murmured. 'We can lie close to the stars and make love to the sound of the sea.'

Her heart was thumping, pounding in her chest. He

took hold of her hand and started to lead the way up the stairs, but before they'd even gone halfway, everything started to go wrong. They both heard the sound of a car on the drive. They stopped, stood very still.

'Who can that be?' she asked. Her mouth was dry and her pulse was beating erratically. 'Do you know anyone who would come out here at this time of night? An emergency call perhaps? Why wouldn't they phone?'

He shook his head. 'I don't know.' He looked as though he was in a daze, caught somewhere between heaven and hell.

The doorbell rang, a sharp and insistent noise as someone pressed the bell repeatedly. José didn't move. It was as if he'd been turned to stone.

Then a woman's voice called out, 'José, I need to talk to you. It's important, please.'

Jessie began to do up the buttons of her dress with shaking fingers. 'You should answer it,' she said quietly. 'It's obviously someone you know and it sounds urgent.'

'It would have to be,' he said in a tight voice, 'to come out here at this time of night.'

Her nerves were on edge, jangling like an out-of-tune orchestra, but she made herself carefully smooth down her dress and then she started to walk back down the stairs. 'Perhaps this was a bad idea, anyway,' she said. After all, how many women were likely to turn up at his door? His grandfather seemed to think there were quite a few. Why would she think she was special?

After a second or two he followed her. 'Do you want to make yourself some coffee,' he suggested, 'while I sort this out?'

She shook her head. 'Whoever she is, she's getting impatient.' The woman was banging on the door now, determined to make herself heard.

He went to the door and opened it. Then he simply stood and stared at the young woman standing in front of him, as though he was stunned.

The woman looked back at him, relief flooding her face. Even in her distress she was clearly a very pretty woman, with cornflower-blue eyes and blond hair falling below her shoulders.

'José, please, I must talk to you,' she said. There was a desperate note to her voice. 'I've been trying to find you for the last couple of hours. I'm so sorry to turn up like this, out of the blue, but I didn't know what else to do. I had to come and see you.'

For a moment he didn't answer, as though he was unable to speak, but then he finally managed to pull himself together.

'Rosanne,' he said in a stunned tone. 'Rosa.'

Jessie's heart gave a gigantic lurch. Rosa? She felt as though her limbs were crumpling beneath her all of a sudden. Wasn't this the girl who José had loved above all others…the girl who had broken his heart, the woman who'd left him for another man? Shivers ran up and down her spine.

'What are you doing here?'

'I needed to see you, José.'

He looked beyond her to where her car was parked. 'Is your husband—is Thomas here with you?' José's voice was thickened, as though he was struggling to get the words out.

'No, I'm here alone,' Rosa said. 'I left him.'

He stared at her, uncomprehending, trying to register what she was saying, and perhaps she realized how taken aback he was because she said, 'I'm sorry, José, really I am. I'm sorry for everything.' She gazed up at him and said on a breathless, ragged note, 'May I come in?'

He didn't answer, but stood back to let her into the hallway. He was acting as though he was in shock, and Jessie couldn't stand it any longer. Her heart was thumping fit to burst.

She had to get out of there. How could she stay here and be the odd one out while José made up with the love of his life?

Quickly, she bent and fumbled to retrieve her bag from where she'd dropped it earlier. She needed to phone for a taxi.

'I'm sorry,' Rosa said, throwing her a quick, nervous glance. 'I'm obviously intruding.'

Jessie shook her head. 'No,' she said in a strained voice. 'It's all right, but I think it's best if I leave. You two seem to have a lot to talk about.' She took her phone from her bag and started to dial the number for a taxi, turning away so that neither of them would see her shaking fingers.

'Jessie, you don't need to do this,' José said quickly, but she could see he'd been thrown by this turn of events. It had knocked him completely out of sync and he was like a man who'd been punched in the stomach.

'I think I do,' she said huskily. She couldn't wait to get out of there. 'Don't worry about it. I think I'll go and wait for my taxi outside—I need to get some air. I'll catch up with you at work on Monday.'

CHAPTER NINE

'YOU'VE HARDLY SAID a word all through breakfast, Jessie.' Ben looked at her across the table. 'What's wrong? Didn't you have a good time at the party last night?'

'The party was great.' She stopped trying to eat her toast. It felt like cardboard in her mouth. 'There were lots of people there, good music—and the food was perfect. There was so much choice.'

'So it has something to do with José.' His eyes narrowed. 'What's he been up to? How has he managed to upset you?'

'He hasn't. Everything's fine.' She stood up and started to pile crockery into the sink. 'I'm fine.'

'No, you're not,' he persisted. 'You left here in a good mood yesterday, and today you look as though your whole world has collapsed.' He frowned. 'You might have played at being his girlfriend but I think you fell for him, big time. And now something's gone wrong. Are you going to see him again—outside work?'

'I...um...I don't know.'

His question had taken her by surprise, and she floundered for a moment or two. When had Ben become so perceptive? He was obviously maturing fast and she hadn't quite been prepared for that.

Ben cursed under his breath. 'You know he has a reputation for being a womanizer, don't you? At least, in the last two or three years or so, I've heard. I tried to tell you. He doesn't get serious about any woman.' He got to his feet and helped to clear the table. 'You're better off without him, Jess.'

'I know. You're probably right.' But it still hurt. José had been completely stunned when Rosanne had turned up on his doorstep and it had been painful to see the warring emotions cross his face. For Jessie's part, it felt as though she'd been cut off at the knees and all she could feel was nausea, a horrible ache deep down in her stomach. 'I should get to work,' she said, abandoning the dishes. 'I'll see you later, Ben.'

Perhaps work would help to take her mind off things. Concentrating on her patients' well-being was the only way she knew to try to counteract this devastating shock to her system.

Gabriel was her first priority. The teenager would be having his surgery later today, and she wanted to find out how he was bearing up before the operation. These past few weeks must have been a difficult time for him and his parents.

He was sitting up in bed on the surgical ward when she stopped by during her morning break. She'd not seen anything of José in the emergency unit so far—he was working with a trauma patient. In a way it was a relief not to have to face him.

'How are you feeling, Gabriel?' she said.

'I'm not too bad, I suppose. They gave me an injection a little while ago, so I'm a bit drowsy.' He frowned. 'The surgeon said the tumour was quite far advanced so he couldn't do the operation by putting a...tube thing... in my nose. I can't remember what he called it.'

'An endoscope. Sometimes doctors can operate that

way, using tiny instruments, but in your case they'll do an incision from the side of your nose.'

'I'm going to look like a freak, aren't I?' His tone was dull. He sounded resigned and disheartened.

'No, no…you won't, I promise.' She could see the fear in his eyes and hurried to reassure him. 'It might leave a faint scar, eventually, but nothing that will damage your good looks.' She smiled at him. 'They're very good at making sure you won't suffer in that way. The only problem for you will be the first two or three weeks after surgery. There will most likely be quite a bit of bruising to your face and you might be worried by that if you aren't expecting it.'

He brightened up. 'I don't mind two or three weeks. I was scared I'd be permanently disfigured.'

'I know. Don't worry about that.'

'Thanks.' He looked relieved. 'Thanks for coming to see me.'

'I wanted to make sure you're okay. I'll come and see you again afterwards, if that's all right?'

'Good. I'd like that.'

She left as his parents came into the room to sit with him. 'I'm glad you came to see him,' his mother said. 'Dr Benitez was here a little while ago. He's been so comforting… You've both been so kind.'

'We're glad to do whatever we can.'

She hurried back to A and E to go on with the day's work. It would be incredibly painful seeing José again, knowing that he might be getting together again with his beloved Rosa, but what could she do? She had to work with him.

'Hi,' Robert said, as she went to check on her list of patients. He was leafing through some files. 'How are you doing?'

'I'm okay,' she said. 'How are things with you?'

'They're good,' he answered cheerfully, and then frowned. 'I'm not so sure about José, though,' he added, looking over to the triage desk where José was standing. 'He seemed a bit distracted first thing this morning—I heard his ex has come back to live over here. It's amazing how rumours and gossip fly around this place. But it must have come as a body blow to him. When I saw him changing into his scrubs he looked as though he'd been steamrollered.'

She sent José a second glance. Fortunately, he didn't appear to have noticed her, because he was talking to a woman who had just come into the unit. She was holding a little boy, about four years old, who was clearly very ill and struggling to breathe.

Even as Jessie watched, it looked as though the child was losing the battle. He suddenly went limp in his mother's arms, and José immediately scooped him up and carried him through to the treatment room.

'I should go and see if he needs any help,' she said, worried by the blue tinge to the child's lips. 'Amanda's gone over to Pathology and the other nurses are busy.'

Robert nodded. 'I'll take the mother to the waiting area and see if I can find someone to sit with her.'

'Thanks.' She hurried over to the treatment room. 'What can I do?' she asked José. He'd already started giving the boy oxygen via nasal tubes and he'd attached leads to a monitor so she could see the child's blood-oxygen level was dangerously low. He was having a severe asthma attack and he wasn't responding when José spoke to him.

'Start him on nebulized salbutamol and ipratroprium bromide—then repeat the treatment every twenty minutes. I'll give him IV hydrocortisone.'

'Okay.'

'How are you feeling, Jack?' he asked the child a few minutes later, but although the boy was conscious now, he wasn't answering. They worked with him for a while longer and then José said tautly, 'He's not responding well enough. We'll start him on IV salbutamol rather than using the nebulizer and we'll set up an infusion— the same with aminophylline. Let's see if that will open up his airways. And we need to get a chest X-ray and blood tests to see if there's an infection bubbling away. I'll start him on antibiotics as a precaution. If all this doesn't make much of a difference, we'll have to get him over to the intensive care unit.'

Eventually, though, Jack at last began to respond to the treatment. His vital signs improved, and his blood-oxygen level started to creep upwards. His breathing slowed a little.

Jessie heaved a sigh of relief. 'Thank heaven.'

José nodded. 'That was a bit too close for comfort.'

'Yes.' She looked at him, recalling the way he'd lifted the child in his arms and carried him in here. He was a caring man, there was no doubt about it. What would he be like with a child of his own? Just thinking about it made a big hollow in her stomach.

Amanda came into the room and said quietly, 'Is everything okay in here? I'll watch over him if you want to go and talk to the parents. His father's just turned up and he's gone to sit with the boy's mother. Oh, and there's someone waiting to see you, José, in the second waiting area.'

'Thanks.' He frowned and turned to Jessie. 'Do you want to walk along with me?' It wasn't really a question. He left the room and held the door open for her to follow him.

'Are you sure you want me to go with you?' Her stomach was churning. She wasn't at all certain she wanted to be with him if Rosanne had turned up at the hospital.

'I'm sure,' he said.

'I mean, if it's Rosa who's waiting for you—I'm not sure I want to be there. You could hardly expect me to want to be a third party while you make up with your ex, could you?'

'Of course not—but it wasn't like that,' he said. 'I'm sorry about what happened, Jessie, but I couldn't turn her away. She was obviously distressed about something and I had to help her. You wouldn't have had me do otherwise, would you?'

'No…I suppose not…but I need to know if she's going to be part of your life from now on. I want to know where I stand.'

'I know. I understand…but she has a lot of problems right now and she needs my help. She's alone now her marriage has broken up and she can't handle things on her own. I need to be there for her.'

'Why? Why should it be you?'

'Because of what we meant to each other in the past.' He frowned. 'She needs me.'

'And where do I fit into all this?'

'You know how I feel about you, Jessie. That hasn't changed.'

'Really?' Somehow she didn't feel comforted. How long would it take Rosa to work her way back into his affections?

They were heading for the room where Jack's parents were waiting, but as they walked along the corridor Jessie was startled to see a familiar figure emerge from the second waiting area.

'Ben—what are you doing here? Are you ill? Is something wrong?'

'Nothing's wrong—except that you're with him,' he said. 'I wish you didn't have to work alongside him. He's bad news.'

She thought back to their conversation that morning. 'Ben, it's all right. You don't need to—'

'I do, Jessie.'

José frowned. 'Let's go back into the relatives' room, shall we? Then you can tell us what the problem is.'

'As if you didn't know.' Ben was angrier than Jessie had seen him in a long time. His face was taut and his green eyes were bright with contempt when he looked at José. Even so, he went back into the room where they could expect some privacy, but as soon as they were in there and the door closed he faced up to José once more.

'Is this about the engravings?' José asked. 'It's been quite a while—but are you angry because I doubted you?'

'It's nothing to do with that, but since you brought it up, you never gave me a chance, did you? From the outset you decided I was to blame. Well, let me tell you, I moved those engravings and put them somewhere safe while the building work was going on. My fingerprints will be all over them if you ever get them back. It proves nothing—'

'As a matter of fact,' José said, 'there's been some good news on that score. I heard from the police early this morning.'

Ben stood stock-still, his head tilted back, while Jessie stared at José, desperate to know what had happened.

'The prints turned up at a special auction yesterday. Luckily, because he'd been advised to look out for them, the sales agent took the precaution of turning on the surveillance cameras and so we have a picture of the man who took them along to be valued.'

Jessie gave a small gasp.

Ben's eyes darkened. 'Who was it? Because it certainly wasn't me,' he said in a terse voice.

'It was one of the men who was subcontracted to the building team. He's been working on properties in the area for some six months and in that time quite a few householders have noticed things going missing, apparently. After the engravings turned up, the agent contacted the police and they arrested him. They searched his house and found a number of stolen items.' He looked at Ben thoughtfully. 'I'm sorry I doubted you, Ben. I was wrong. I apologize.'

'You can keep your apologies. What do I care?' Ben's tone was scathing. 'I'd done nothing wrong—I knew it. My conscience was clear. But you...' His eyes blazed. 'Your crime is far worse. You hurt my sister. I don't know exactly what went on between you, but I know you upset her and she doesn't deserve that.'

José glanced at Jessie, his blue eyes unfathomable. 'I've no intention of hurting your sister. I would never willingly do that.'

Jessie wished the floor would swallow her up. 'Ben, please, you don't need to do this.' She was desperate to stop him. It would be far better for her if José knew nothing of the extent to which he'd hurt her. It was embarrassing...humiliating.

'I do, Jess. I won't have him upsetting you.' He turned his attention back to José. 'I'm warning you now, if you so much as touch her, you'll regret it.'

José acknowledged him with a brief nod. 'I'm sorry if I've upset Jessie. I would never want to do that.'

Ben glowered at him. 'Just bear in mind that you'll

deal with me if you ever do.' He looked at Jessie. 'But you let me know if you have any bother from him.' He checked his watch. 'I have to go, Jess. I'll see you later at the reef, won't I?'

'Yes, that's right. I'm on duty there today.'

He left the room and she closed her eyes in mortification. He'd meant well, but she wished he hadn't turned up here.

'He shouldn't have said what he did,' she said, glancing briefly at José.

'He was trying to protect you—that's good,' José said. 'I'm glad you have him to look out for you.'

'Yes, I'm thankful for that…and that was good news about the prints,' she murmured, wanting to get onto safer ground. 'Your patience paid off in the end.'

'It did.' He looked at her searchingly. 'Jessie…about last night…I'm sorry things turned out the way they did.'

'I suppose it couldn't be helped.' She sent him a brief glance. 'Is Rosanne back for good?'

'It's possible.' He frowned. 'She says her marriage has broken down and she's come here to stay with her parents. Apparently she arrived on the island a few days ago.'

'Oh, I see.' And the first person she'd turned to had been José. That said it all, didn't it?

His pager went off just then and he quickly read the text message. His expression grew more and more serious as he scanned the words.

'What's wrong? Is Jack all right?'

'It isn't about Jack. It's Gabriel—he's had a bad bleed during surgery. They're having to give him a transfusion.'

'Oh, no…' Her heart sank. 'I thought with the embolization he would be safe from that?'

'Obviously not. It doesn't carry a guarantee that there won't be a bleed, not in serious cases, anyway.' He looked worried, preoccupied, and Jessie felt the same way, her anxiety growing for the teenager.

Her own pager went off and she quickly read the message. 'I have to go—an emergency patient has just been brought in.'

'Okay.' He lightly touched her arm as she turned away. 'We'll talk later?'

She nodded…but what was there to say? He'd found his true love again. He wasn't likely to let her go a second time, was he, given the chance to make things right?

She walked away from him and went to see to her patients, dealing with fractures and feverish illnesses and various other kinds of emergencies until her shift finished late in the afternoon. She tried to keep out of José's way. He clouded her thinking and wrenched her heart with unbearable sadness.

She went straight to the coral reef from her work at the hospital, taking the motor launch laid on for visitors. Up till now, she'd done a couple of stints there without José and she was getting used to the kind of incidents that occurred. There was rarely anything major, but she had her full kit with her should anything adverse happen.

Ben was already getting ready for his dive when she arrived and stepped onto the yacht. He acknowledged her with a thumbs-up sign and she smiled in return.

'Hi,' the skipper said. 'Glad to have you on board, Doc.'

'I'm glad to be here,' she answered. 'Are there any problems?'

'Not so far.'

She went over to the group of divers and made some basic checks before they started suiting up. 'Okay, you're good to go,' she said.

They finished getting ready, checking their equipment, and then one by one they descended into the water.

'They're not going too deep today,' the skipper told her. 'I expect they'll be down there for about half an hour.' He smiled. 'Time for you to sit back and enjoy the scenery. I'll get you a cool drink.'

'Thanks.'

She did as he suggested, gazing out across the blue water at the ridge of land beyond. She sipped her cold drink and tried not to think of José, but it was impossible. Her mind kept wandering and she thought back to the times she had spent here with him…good times, when they'd been on his yacht and he'd pointed out the beauties of the landscape, the birds that flew overhead, or the more adventurous types that landed on the guard rail.

And then, as though she had conjured him up, here he was, coming across the water towards her, standing at the helm of his yacht, his shirt riffling in the breeze. She blinked and when she realized she wasn't seeing things, her pulse quickened. Why was he here?

He came on board a couple of minutes later, exchanging greetings with the skipper. 'Are you doing an extra shift?' the skipper said jokingly.

'I'm just here to help out,' José answered. He sat down next to Jessie. 'I thought we should talk,' he said quietly. 'I feel bad about last night ending the way it did.'

'Rosa was obviously distressed,' she murmured. 'You did what you had to do.'

'I'm glad you understand.'

She gave an awkward shrug. 'I'm not sure I do, fully. She said she loved you and then walked out on you, and yet you seem prepared to welcome her into your home as though nothing had happened.' Perhaps he was simply a caring, sensitive man who couldn't stand by and see a woman in distress without wanting to help out. It was upsetting and confusing and it hurt her head thinking about it.

'I didn't feel I had any choice.'

'Will you be seeing her again?'

A muscle in his jaw flinched. 'I think it's inevitable. Her circumstances have changed and she's back here to stay with her parents. I'm not—'

She never heard what he was about to say because there was a disturbance in the water just then and one of the divers emerged, supporting one of the other men. He helped him over to the guardrail and called for the skipper to come over.

'There's something wrong with him,' he said. 'It's his chest, I think. He was coming up too quickly and there's a problem with his breathing.'

José and the skipper rushed over to the side of the yacht and hauled the young man aboard. Jessie looked on, horrified when she saw that it was her brother who was the one in difficulty.

José carefully removed the mask and breathing apparatus from him and Ben started to cough, clutching at his chest. He was doubled over with pain, finding it difficult to breathe, and when he coughed again Jessie was alarmed to see a trickle of blood coming from his mouth.

She grabbed her medical kit and knelt down beside him. 'I'm going to give you some oxygen,' she said. José had already gone to fetch the oxygen cylinder from the first-aid bay on board the yacht. Connecting it up, she put the mask over Ben's face and mouth. He coughed and spluttered, but tried to breathe in the life-giving gas.

She quickly examined him, alarmed by the way his windpipe was distorted and the blood vessels in his neck were standing out. She guessed what must have happened.

As he had come up through the water, tiny air sacs in his lungs must have expanded, and because he'd ascended too quickly, or perhaps because his oxygen tank had been out of air—maybe a faulty gauge, or he hadn't checked the tank properly—these sacs had burst. The air had escaped into the pleural cavity surrounding the lung and now it was filling it up like a balloon, causing it to press on the lung and deflate it.

'His lung has collapsed,' she told José. 'I need to do a thoracostomy.' If she didn't act fast, his air supply would be compromised even more and he could go into shock and then suffer a cardiac arrest.

He nodded. 'I'll swab the area for you.'

'Thanks.'

They worked together, and all the time she tried to reassure Ben, who was near collapse. 'I'm going to inject you with an anaesthetic so you shouldn't feel any pain,' she told him, 'and then I'll put in a chest tube to release the pressure and allow your lung to re-inflate.'

She started the procedure, injecting him and then carefully feeling for the space between his ribs where she needed to introduce the tube. Once it was in place, there was a small rush of air, and she capped off the end of the tube with a flutter valve to stop the air seeping back in.

'How are you feeling, Ben?' she asked.

'Much better,' he said. 'The pain's nowhere near as bad, and I can breathe now.'

'That's good. I'll tape the tube in place and put a dressing on your wound and then we'll get you to hospital.'

He coughed and winced, and Jessie bit her lip. He was already bleeding into his lung and if he coughed too much they could have another emergency on their hands. They needed to get him to A and E right now.

'We'll take him on the yacht,' José said. 'My car's at

the quayside, so we should be at the hospital in less than half an hour. I'll call ahead and tell them to expect us.'

'Thanks.' She turned to the skipper. 'We need the stretcher,' she said, and he hurried away with another of the divers, returning with it almost immediately.

'Well done, Doc,' he said. 'You did a great job there.'

She gave him a weak smile. This was her brother, and she couldn't be as detached from his situation as she might have been with a stranger. She knew the dangers of his situation and she was worried sick.

José and the skipper carried Ben on board his yacht and made sure he was comfortable and secure in the cabin. 'It won't be long now,' José told him. 'We'll have you safe on dry land before you know it.'

The skipper left them and waved them off from the dive boat, and Jessie went to sit with her brother. José stood at the helm once more and guided the yacht towards their destination, giving it as much speed as possible.

Robert and his team met them at the ambulance bay. 'We'll take care of him from here,' he told Jessie. 'We'll check him over and get some X-rays done. Why don't you go and wait in José's office and I'll let you know what's happening? You can't do anything more now.'

'But I should be with him,' Jessie protested.

'No, Robert's right,' José said, putting his arm around her and turning her away. 'Leave them to do their job. You've done your bit—you saved his life.'

'I hope so. I hope he's going to be all right.' She went with him to his office and once they were in there she began to pace the room restlessly.

'You'll wear yourself out,' he said, putting his arms around her and holding her tight. 'He'll be fine with Robert and his team. They haven't lost any patients—

not today, at least.' He gave her an encouraging smile
and she gave a choked laugh at his attempt at humour.

'How can you joke at a time like this?' she said with a
shake of her head. 'It's my brother we're talking about.'

'I know…but they say laughter's the best medicine,
don't they? And I really believe he'll be all right.'

She nodded and buried her head into the comforting
warmth of his chest. She felt safe in his arms, as though
he would protect her from the outside world. Was that
possible?

There was a knock at the door, and she eased herself
away from him. Reluctantly, he let her go, looking at her
searchingly before he went to see who was demanding
his attention.

The door opened and Amanda came into the room.
'There's someone here to see you, José,' she said. 'Is it
all right to bring her in?'

José looked beyond her to where Rosanne stood waiting in the corridor. Every nerve cell in Jessie's body
began to scream. This couldn't be happening, not now.
Not again. How did this woman manage to intrude on
every private, intimate moment? Why did José allow it?

But it seemed he was going to go along with whatever
she wanted. 'Yes. Come in, Rosa,' he said.

Jessie reached for a chair and sat down, all the strength
draining from her. This time she wasn't going to run
away. He could decide once and for all who it was that
he wanted, her or Rosa.

There was another shock in store for her, though.
When Rosa came into the room, she wasn't alone. She
had with her a small boy, around three or four years
old. He was a sweet-faced child, a bit shy, but looking
around with a natural inquisitiveness. He was pale and
perhaps a little thin, but what was most striking about

him was that he had black hair and wide blue eyes. It was those features that made Jessie look from him to José and back again.

Jessie watched the boy carefully, trying to work out the timeline in her head. Could he be José's child? José had said he'd bought his boat about three years ago, so it was possible Rosa had already been pregnant with his child when she'd left him.

Rosa looked across the room at Jessie. 'I'm interrupting again,' she said flatly. 'I'm sorry. It's just that my little boy is poorly and I need to ask José for help. He has a congenital heart problem,' she explained. 'José has been so kind and I didn't know who else to turn to.' She lifted her gaze to him and said softly, 'But I could leave, if this is the wrong time…'

She started to turn away, but José reached out to her and touched her arm. 'No, Rosa, it's all right. Please, stay.' He gently steered her to a chair. 'Sit down.' Then he laid a hand lightly on the toddler's shoulder. 'You, too, Mattie. There are some toys in a box in the corner. Go and help yourself.'

Mattie brightened up at the mention of toys and went to sit at the low table where model cars and building blocks were already set out.

'I'll make some coffee,' José said, going over to the machine at the side of the room.

'Not for me,' Jessie told him quietly. Seeing him gently lay his hand on Rosa's arm had been the final crushing blow for her. 'I need to go and phone my father and tell him what's happened to Ben.'

José frowned. 'Yes, of course. He'll want to know. Come back when you're ready.'

She nodded, but she knew she wouldn't go back. She

left his office and went outside to make her call in the open air.

Too many things were happening all at once and she needed some space and time to think. What did José feel for Rosa after all this time? Did he still love her?

Perhaps she could have won the battle for his affections if it had just been Rosa she'd had to contend with… but Rosa had something Jessie could never match. She had the child.

If it turned out that Mattie was José's son, there would be no contest. Rosa had already won hands down.

CHAPTER TEN

THE SOUND OF childish laughter was the first thing Jessie heard as she entered A and E the next morning. Then, as she walked towards one of the treatment bays, she saw José standing by the window, holding Mattie in his arms. The little one was laughing through his fingers at something José was saying, while his mother looked on. Rosanne was gazing up at José and smiling.

Jessie looked at them and felt her heart turn over. Everything she'd dreamed of was in that little tableau… except she wasn't a part of it. The child wasn't hers and she wasn't the woman that José wanted in his life. It was unbearable to stand here and watch them, yet for a moment or two she couldn't tear herself away.

How could she ever have thought José might want her above all women? It had been a fantasy, a piece of wishful thinking that could never come about. And it hurt to have her dreams shattered.

She'd never felt this way about her ex. True, she'd been upset when she found he'd cheated on her, but there hadn't been this heart-rending sense of loss, this feeling that she would never recover from such a betrayal. And now here she was, desperately wishing she'd never met José and fallen under his spell.

She walked away and tried to blot the image from

her mind, but as she headed over to the triage area she caught sight of Robert looking at her, an odd expression clouding his eyes.

'Are you all right?' he asked as she approached the desk.

'Yes, of course. Why wouldn't I be?'

He shifted uneasily, straightening his shoulders. 'I saw you looking in on José just now. I tried to warn you, way back when you first came here…do you remember? I was afraid you might fall for him, but it happened, didn't it?'

'There's no one to blame for that but myself. Like you say, I went in with my eyes wide open.' She made a rueful face. 'I should have known better.' She glanced towards the treatment bay. 'Do you have any idea why they're here—Rosanne and her little boy?'

'I think she's been worried about the child being unwell—he's due to have a procedure soon to repair a heart defect, and she was afraid the doctors wouldn't be able to go ahead with it.'

'Oh, I see.' The child had been pale and a bit smaller than might have been expected, but that was often the case with children who had heart problems. She felt so sorry for that child. Life wasn't fair, sometimes. 'Well, I expect José has managed to put her mind at rest. They look happy enough, anyway.'

Trying to keep busy, she picked up a file from the desk and began to scan the pages. 'I should go and see to my patients,' she murmured. In a momentary pause she gave a wistful glance around. 'I'll miss this place when I leave. I've learned so much, seen so many youngsters that we've been able to help.'

But she couldn't go on working here, could she, not now that things looked to be going so disastrously wrong between her and José?

Robert looked stricken. 'I'd forgotten you were only here for a short time. We'll have to do something about that. I'm not sure that the colleague you're here to cover for will be coming back—and even if she does, we need another paediatrician. We'll find a way for you to stay.'

She shook her head. 'I don't think so. Anyway, I must get on.' She held up the file she'd been reading. 'I've a small patient with a thread twisted around his toe that no one seems to be able to remove. Apparently the toe is red and swollen.'

He blinked. 'How are you going to deal with that one?'

She smiled. 'With ingenuity, patience and a lot of help from anaesthesia and a scalpel, most likely.'

He chuckled. 'Sounds as though you know what you're doing. Rather you than me.'

She spent the rest of the morning tending to her patients, and finally managed to grab a break for lunch when the queue of waiting patients died down.

José caught up with her in the hospital restaurant. 'You didn't come back to the office yesterday,' he said as he slid into a chair opposite her. 'I waited for you and then tried to find you but you'd disappeared.' He frowned. 'I was worried. You weren't answering your phone either.'

'No, it had been a long day, so I switched it off.' The truth was, she hadn't wanted to talk to José. She didn't know what to think, and even if she asked him what he felt for Rosa now that she was here on the island, she didn't expect a straight answer. How could he know what he wanted right now? His emotions were probably all over the place, unless he was the out-and-out womanizer that Ben had painted.

'I went to see Ben once he was settled on the ward,' she told him. 'Then I drove over to my father's house.

I decided it might be better to break the news to him in person.'

'I suppose that was the best idea. How did he take it?'

She pulled a face. 'He was shocked. I think even Hollie was concerned. It brings it home to you the value of family and relationships, doesn't it, when things like this happen?'

'Yes, that's true.' He slid a fork into his lasagne. 'So, is he going to visit him now that he's in hospital?'

She nodded. 'He's with him right now. They're keeping Ben here for a while until it's safe to remove the chest tube and they're giving him supplemental oxygen and antibiotics to clear up any infection.'

'Does he know how it happened? What caused the barotrauma?'

'The skipper said he must have run out of air—there was a small rupture in the hose. He says Ben might have scraped against something sharp while he was underwater.'

José sucked in his breath. 'That was nasty—a freak accident. In a way he was lucky they weren't doing a deep dive—he wouldn't have made it back up to the surface.'

'I know.' She pushed her plate away and took a sip of coffee. She wanted to know what was going on between him and Rosa, but she was almost afraid to ask, so she sidestepped the issue. 'Robert told me that Rosa's child has to have an operation. I saw you with the little boy this morning.' She tried a smile. 'He seems to have taken to you.'

He chuckled. 'Yes, I guess so.'

'What kind of heart problem does he have? Rosanne is obviously very concerned about him.'

'He was born with a hole in the heart, but it only started causing him problems in the last year. He gets tired easily and suffers a lot of respiratory infections, and lately his legs have started to swell. The doctors decided it's time it was sorted out before it causes him permanent damage.'

'Poor little thing.' She'd come across this type of illness before several times—in the womb, the baby had an opening between the upper chambers of the heart, but this usually closed after birth. If it didn't close, too much oxygen-rich blood would be pumped to the lungs, causing a rise in pressure, and less oxygenated blood would go out to the rest of the body tissues. The increased blood flow to the lungs would create a swishing sound, a heart murmur that could be heard through a stethoscope. 'It's no wonder Rosa's upset.'

'Yes. That's why she turned to me for help.'

She looked at him from under her lashes. 'Would that be medical help she's looking for, or emotional support?'

'A bit of both, I think.' He finished his lasagne and reached for his coffee. 'She's floundering a bit, between the problems of his illness, the medical opinions, insurance claims and the fact that her marriage has hit a rock. She seems a bit lost, and that's why she's clinging to me, so to speak.'

'But even if her marriage has broken down, surely you would expect her and her husband to support each other through something like this?' Unless, of course, the husband hadn't fathered the child. That would put a different slant on things.

'You'd think so, wouldn't you?'

'But instead of looking to him for help, she came to you—how do you feel about that? You were definitely taken aback to begin with.' Now, though, he appeared to be more than willing to stand by her. It was the honourable thing to do, but he wasn't doing this out of duty, was he? He was emotionally involved.

'I'm not sure how I feel. This is not something I expected and I'm trying to deal with it one day at a time.' He looked at her steadily. 'I'm sorry about the other night.' He gave a rueful smile. 'The timing was way off.'

Her shoulders lifted a fraction. 'Maybe not so much. It gave me something to think about. After all, I made a mistake once before—I don't want to do the same again.'

His eyes darkened. 'It wasn't a mistake, Jessie—surely you don't believe that?'

'I believe that what's going on between you and Rosa isn't over. She needs you and you're there for her. Perhaps you always will be.'

She stood up and started to pile her used crockery onto a tray. 'I must go—I want to look in on Ben before my afternoon shift starts and maybe find time to check up on Jack and Gabriel.'

'I'll go with you.'

'No. Stay and finish your dessert. I need to get a move on. I'm hoping my father will still be on the ward by the time I get there.' She knew he didn't want her to go without him, and perhaps he wanted to reassure her that all would be well between them, but she couldn't know how long that would last. Rosa had come back and everything had changed.

She hurried away, the thought of José and Rosa in each other's arms playing over and over in her mind, like a recurring nightmare. She couldn't shake it off.

It was a relief to find her father was still at Ben's bedside when she walked onto the ward. He greeted her with an awkward smile. 'I'm glad you told me what happened,' he said. 'After the way your last visit went I didn't think I'd hear from you again.'

'Things didn't go too well, did they?' She gave a light shrug, going over to the bed and giving Ben's hand a gentle squeeze. Glancing back at her father, she said, 'He's your son. I thought it only right that you should know what was going on.'

'Yes,' He sighed heavily. 'I've handled things badly, haven't I? It's not that I wanted all this upset between us. I have a quick temper…and so does Ben.' He glanced at her brother. 'I'm sorry for the things I said. I should have listened to you, thought more about how you were feeling about everything. You're my flesh and blood and I shouldn't have thrown you out. I put you in an impossible situation, with the job and everything.'

Ben's eyes narrowed. 'What's brought on this turnabout? You didn't have any qualms about it before.'

Jessie watched as a series of conflicting expressions crossed her father's face. He seemed to be struggling to find the right words.

'The thing is, with Hollie,' he said awkwardly, 'she's very insecure. I try to look out for her and do my best for her, but it's somehow clouded my judgement. I realize that now.' He shot Ben a quick glance. 'When I thought I could have lost you I knew that I had to make some changes. You're my son. It's time I made up to you for those lost years.'

He turned to Jessie. 'And those things I said to you—it was the heat of the moment. I'm not a saint, I get stressed, with the business, the workload, the demands everyone makes of me…and I hit out. I know you're doing a worthwhile job. You were there for Ben when he needed you. You've always been there for him, and—' He broke off. 'It's not easy for me to say this, but…I'm ashamed of the way I've behaved towards both of you.'

Jessie threw him a cautious glance. 'I'd like to think things might change.'

He nodded. 'They will.' He looked at Ben. 'You could come back to live at the house, have your job back.'

Ben shook his head. 'I don't think so. I don't think it would work. Like you say, we're both hot-headed and we wouldn't last a week under the same roof without falling out. And Hollie needs some space.' He paused, struggling a little for breath. 'I'm happy living at the apartment, and I've discovered I'm enjoying the job I'm doing. I think I'll take it up seriously and get some qualifications, maybe even start my own business one day. My boss thinks I'll be good enough. So, thanks...but, no, thanks.'

It was clear her father was stunned by what Ben had said, but he looked at him with new eyes. 'Okay,' he said. 'I understand how you feel. Maybe you'll let me support you in your studies—help you out with fees, and so on.'

'Wow.' Ben laughed. 'Now, there's an offer well worth thinking about.'

Jessie said goodbye to both of them a short time later and went back to work. She checked up on Jack, the four-year-old who'd had the nasty asthma attack, and found that he was doing well. His vital signs had improved considerably and the antibiotics were working to deal with the underlying infection that had caused the problem to erupt. The respiratory specialist had decided he would keep an eye on him on a regular basis.

Gabriel wasn't in such good shape. He was uncomfortable after the surgery and he was pale and exhausted after losing a lot of blood. She spoke to him for a while and tried to reassure him, but he was tired and in the end she left him to try to get some sleep.

Mattie's heart procedure was scheduled for the next day, and Jessie found that the little boy was on her mind a lot of the time over the next few hours. How must José be feeling if Mattie really was his child? It was no wonder he was distracted and needed to take things one step at a time.

Jessie went into work the following morning and came across José coming out of one of the treatment bays. He was talking on the phone, apparently checking on arrangements for Mattie's treatment.

'Is everything on schedule?' Jessie asked him when he'd finished the call.

He nodded. 'It will all be over by late this afternoon,' he said. 'They're going to prep him at lunchtime, and the whole thing will take a couple of hours.'

'He won't be having open-heart surgery, then?'

'No, thankfully not. He's going to have a catheter intervention.' He winced. 'It's still a scary procedure as far as the parents are concerned, though.'

'I imagine it is.' She couldn't help wondering how he was feeling. He looked okay, but as a doctor he would probably be used to controlling his emotions where patients were concerned.

In this instance Mattie would be anaesthetized and then the surgeon would make a small incision in his groin. A thin tube would be passed through a vein all the way up to his heart, and then a device would be inserted through the tube. When the device was in place next to the hole in the heart, the tube would be withdrawn and the device would open up like an umbrella and flatten itself against the hole. The pumping of the heart would keep it in place initially, but in time the heart tissue would grow around the device so that it became a permanent fixture.

'It's generally thought of as a very safe procedure,' she murmured by way of comfort.

'Yes. But I don't think Rosa is convinced of that. I told her I would go and see her when they take him into the catheterization unit and I might bring her down here to the office while it's going on. Robert said he would cover for me here. I owe him one.'

'I hope it goes well.'

'Thanks, Jessie.' He looked at his watch. 'In the meantime, I have a few more patients to see.' He touched her arm briefly, sending myriad sensations to scatter in chaotic disorder throughout her body. Her heart made a strange flip over. But then he hurried away, leaving her to mourn the loss of that fleeting contact. What did he feel for her? He'd never really talked about love, except to hint at it, and perhaps that was impossible for him, given the past.

She worked through the morning, taking time out during a coffee break to go and see Gabriel. He was looking much more cheerful than the last time she'd seen him.

'Hi,' he said, trying to give her a grin as best he could through the mass of dressings on his face. 'I look a mess, don't I?'

'I'm sure you're still as good-looking as ever underneath it all,' she said with a laugh in response. 'You're obviously feeling better today. There's more colour in your cheeks—what I can see of them.'

'Yeah. The surgeon told me he got all of the tumour out, but they'll do a follow-up radiotherapy treatment to mop things up. José reckons in another three or four weeks, I'll be good to go.'

She smiled. 'The girls had better watch out then. Gabriel is back!'

'Yay!' They made a high five, and Jessie stayed for a little while longer until his parents came to visit him.

For the next few of hours she worked her way steadily

through her list of patients, treating a girl with a broken collarbone and sending a child who had swallowed a button battery to the endoscopy unit to have it removed from his stomach.

'You missed lunch,' Robert said, looking in on her as she put the last stitch in a gash on a child's foot. 'It's way past time you went off to get something to eat. We're okay here,' he said with a smile. 'It's quiet for the time being, so make the best of it.'

'All right. As soon as I've finished here I'll grab a sandwich and go and see my brother. He's being discharged today, so I'll be able to collect him and drive him home after work.'

'That's good news.'

'Yes.'

She gave her patient a smiley sticker and left him and his mother in Amanda's care.

Walking past José's office, she glanced through the open door to see if he was there. Mattie's procedure should be over fairly soon, and she wondered if José and Rosa had gone back up to the catheterization unit. No doubt a nurse would page José when they were almost ready.

They were still in his office, though, and perhaps that call had just come through, because José checked his pager and then stood up. He said something and Rosa suddenly went pale and began to tremble. She put out a hand to touch his chest, palm flat, and he wrapped his arms around her and held her close to him.

Jessie watched them, frozen to the spot. José didn't seem worried by the message on his pager, so surely nothing could have gone badly wrong? Why was it necessary for him to hold her like that?

Her stomach was churning, her blood raging with jealousy, and through it all she felt deeply ashamed of herself for reacting this way. Rosa was going through a trying, horrible experience, with her son in such a fragile condition. Why couldn't she accept that, and accept that she needed comfort?

But it didn't seem to matter that there were logical reasons why he should be holding her. Her mind rejected them all and raged at the thought of another woman in his arms. Her temples were throbbing madly, and her nails bit into her palms as she squeezed her hands into fists by her side.

'Jessie?' José saw her and after a second's hesitation held Rosa at arm's length.

'I'm on my way to see Ben,' she said hurriedly, determined not to give herself away, and then on a worried note added, 'I hope everything's all right with Mattie?'

'A slight arrhythmia started up after the procedure. They're keeping an eye on him. It happens sometimes.'

'Yes, that's right. It does.' She would comfort any woman fearful for her son—she just didn't see why in José's case it had to involve them in a clinch. 'I'm sure he'll be fine.'

She walked away quickly, going out into the corridor and taking the lift up to Ben's ward. She didn't bother with food. It would taste like straw right now.

'How are you?' she asked Ben, as she approached his bedside. She'd spoken with the nurse and she'd confirmed he was doing well.

'I'm a lot better,' he told her. 'They said I could go home as long as my temperature is okay and my blood pressure is stable.'

'That's right. You'll need to rest for a while at home for a few days, but your boss is all right with that, isn't he?'

'Yeah. He's been really good through all this.' He

looked around. 'I can't wait to get out of here. No offence, I know it's your work and all that, but...'

She smiled. 'None taken. I know what you mean.' She glanced at his holdall and all the bits and pieces on his bedside locker. 'I'll start to pack up your things, shall I? Then I'll leave you to get dressed and come back for you later when my shift finishes. I brought you a paper to read while you're waiting.'

'Thanks, Jess. You're an angel.' He shot her a quick glance. 'How are things with you and José? Has he said anything about what happens when your contract here comes to an end?'

'We're all right.' She started to fold clothes from the locker and put them in his overnight bag, leaving a clean pair of jeans and a T-shirt for him to put on. 'No, he hasn't mentioned it, but I think I'm going to start applying for jobs.' She thought it over. 'Maybe I'll look for something on one of the other islands where they have A and E units like this one. That way, I'll still be close enough to come and see you and Dad.' And far enough away from José to be sure she wouldn't run into him.

His eyes narrowed. 'Wouldn't they be able to find you a job here? Strikes me they could use a few more doctors in A and E, from what you've told me.'

'I doubt it. Anyway, it'll be good to see what life's like somewhere else. And I'll still be able to keep an eye on you.'

He laughed. 'Sure. Like I'm ever going to be able to get away with anything!'

She left him to get dressed and went back to the emergency department to finish her shift. Thankfully, José was nowhere to be seen and Robert told her he was working with a patient who'd had a stroke.

'Rosanne's in the recovery ward with her little boy. She'll be able to take him home later today.'

'I'm glad he's all right.'

Just before her shift ended she managed to download a few interesting jobs that were advertised on the internet, along with a couple of application forms that she printed out. She would spend the weekend going through them and see if she could put together a good argument as to why they should take her on.

Painful as it was to leave, she wouldn't stay here and weep over José. He'd somehow managed to make her fall in love with him, but he'd never told her that he loved her. Was she just another possible conquest? Or had everything gone wrong because Rosa had turned up?

Now he had to make up his mind about what he really wanted. She wasn't going to stay around while he came to a decision.

CHAPTER ELEVEN

'DO YOU THINK I'll be able to dive again fairly soon?' Ben asked the next day, as he watched Jessie put the finishing touches to a salad she was making. It was the weekend and she was supposed to be relaxing alongside him, but she had this insatiable urge to keep busy.

'It wouldn't be safe for you to dive until your chest has completely healed,' she said, 'and you'd have to be declared medically fit before you were allowed near any scuba-diving equipment, to be honest.' She saw the downward tilt of his mouth and tacked on quickly, 'But you're young, strong and otherwise fit, so it shouldn't be too long before you're back in your diving gear.' She added grilled shrimp to a bed of salad leaves that she'd mixed with wedges of avocado and mango. 'I can't see any reason why you shouldn't swim, though.'

'Yeah. I could do that.' He smiled. 'I could always turn up at Dad's place with my swimming trunks and towel and say I've come for a dip in the pool. How do you think that would go down?'

She laughed. 'Pretty well at the moment, I should think.' She made a lime and cilantro dressing, adding mustard, adobo sauce, canola oil and a touch of honey. 'I'll put this in the fridge and we can have it later.' Wiping her hands, she said musingly, 'I want to spend some time looking over the application forms I downloaded and see what's to be done. What do you have planned for the rest of the day? Nothing strenuous, I hope?'

'No. I thought I might go over and hang out with Tim—you know him from the dive site, don't you? He's the one who had a brush with a sea urchin.'

'Yes, I know Tim. I like him… I'm glad you and he get on well.'

He sent her a quizzical look. 'You're not going to spend all afternoon filling in those forms, are you? You're in the Caribbean, Jess—there are all sorts of good things you could be doing.'

'I suppose you're right.' She thought about it. 'Actually, I might go for a walk on the beach later. There's a bit down by the rocks that I haven't explored yet.'

'See that you do.' He got to his feet and started to head out of the door, but then he stopped and said, 'You seem to be really keen on going ahead with these applications. Is there no changing your mind? I'll bet you haven't even looked at the options at the hospital where you are now.'

'Perhaps I need a change.'

'Hmm.'

He went out and Jessie cleared up after her salad-making session and wiped down the worktop. Both jobs on offer seemed to be the kind of thing she was looking for. Her qualifications were good and the experience she'd just had at the Mount Saint Helene hospital was probably exactly what they were looking for. She had to at least make an effort to go after them.

She spent some time carefully filling in both forms and then put them in envelopes ready to go in the post once she'd added the ID photos they wanted. Then she locked up the apartment and set off for the nearby cove that she hadn't yet had time to explore properly.

She followed a well-worn footpath through the trees that shaded the land near the apartments. There was a fairly steep descent down to the beach from here, with steps built into the cliff face at one point, leading to a long stretch of golden sand. It was beautiful here, tranquil, with coconut palms and sea-grape trees casting much-needed shade from the glowing heat of the sun, but despite the calmness of her surroundings, Jessie's mind was far from being still.

It seemed there was a thorny scrub patch in paradise that stopped her from taking pleasure in this beautiful place. And José was at the centre of it, with his charm and resourcefulness, his gentle ways and his sensual touch. He'd worked his way into her emotions and now she rued the day she'd ever met him. Her peace of mind had been shattered forever.

She walked along the warm sand, lifting her gaze to the jagged shoreline, where the promontory broke up into a rugged cliff face, with scattered rocky outcrops and pools left by the outgoing tide. Here and there starfish lay, abandoned, and colourful birds came down to the shoreline to investigate any tasty pickings.

She sat down on the flattest rock she could find and gazed out at the crystal-clear turquoise waters to the distant coral reef. Perhaps she would never go there again with José. Soon that might be all in the past.

'Jessie…at last. I've been trailing you for the last few minutes.' José's voice came to her out of the blue and she turned to look at him in surprise. Her heart made a small leap. She was more than glad to see him, and yet she was disturbed at the same time. He said quietly, 'You must have been miles away in your head, deep in thought.'

'Yes, I was.' She sent him a puzzled look. 'I would

never have expected to see you here. Were you looking for me?'

'I was.'

'How did you know where to find me?'

'Ben told me where to look.'

'Ben?' She frowned. 'But how could he have done that? He's gone to see his friend Tim.'

He shrugged. 'He may have gone there now, but he came to see me first.' He studied her thoughtfully. 'He seems to be quite worried about you.'

'Is he? I can't think why.'

'He cares for you very much.' He sat down beside her on the rock.

She nodded. 'I know. The feeling's mutual.' She frowned, suddenly on edge. 'I hope he didn't cause you any trouble. Is that why you're here—because of something he said?'

'In a way, yes. He told me you were planning on leaving. He thought I should know about it. Is it true?'

'I'm thinking about it, yes. When the contract at the hospital comes to an end I'll need to find something else. So I've been taking a look at some options.' She picked up some shells from the sand around her, brushing off the grains with her fingers and dropping them into her lap.

'You don't need to look for another job, Jessie. I could find a permanent post for you at Mount Saint Helene.'

'You came after me to offer me a job?'

'No, *chica*, I came to find out why you're thinking of leaving when you and I were getting on so well together. I thought we had something going between us, and yet you've made up your mind to walk out on me. Don't I deserve some kind of explanation?'

'I'm not sure.' She sent him a troubled look. 'The way I see things, you also have something going with Rosa.'

His brows drew together. 'That was over a long time ago.'

'Was it? Perhaps Rosa needs to be reminded of that.'

He stared at her, apparently uncomprehending. 'Why would you say that? She's been worried about Mattie and she needed someone to turn to. Why would she not come to me? Am I supposed to turn her away because we're no longer together?'

'No, of course not. I understand that you want to do whatever you can for her. But are you sure it's really over between you? She's upset about her son's illness, I can see that, but she seems to be turning to you for a bit more than advice and support.'

He looked at her steadily. 'You saw me holding her, comforting her, and that upset you?'

'It did. How would you feel if Robert put his arms around me?'

'Murderous.' He stiffened. 'You're not thinking of letting him do that, are you?'

She ignored his question and countered with one of her own. 'Do you understand what I'm trying to say? Of course it bothers me. I told you I'd been hurt once before, José. I've had enough of men who cheat and lie and I'm not going down that route again, ever.'

He put his arm around her waist and she tried to shrug him off. 'I can't let you persuade me that everything's all right when it's not,' she said.

'It's not the way you think,' he said, drawing her close to him. 'Rosa's always been a bit needy. I suspect that's what went wrong between her and her husband. He's away a lot and she couldn't cope with it, especially once she found out that Mattie was ill.'

'I'm surprised he wasn't here to be with his child at a time like this—unless, of course, he isn't Mattie's real father.' She looked up at him, daring him to tell the truth. 'You and she would have been together when Mattie was conceived wouldn't you? Or do I have the timing wrong?'

His mouth made a wry curve. 'You've been thinking about this a lot, haven't you?'

She nodded.

'Well, you're absolutely right about that. She was with me when Mattie was conceived.' His gaze meshed with hers. 'But he's not my child. The truth is, she cheated on me and when I found out about it we had a parting of the ways.'

Jessie's face flushed with colour. 'I'm so sorry. That must have been devastating for you.' At the same time, she was beginning to feel better already. A little glow of warmth started up inside her. Mattie wasn't his child.

'My pride was hurt, I'll admit. But we'd been drifting apart for quite some time. I think the break-up was a relief in the end.'

'Really?' She frowned. She wanted to believe him, but… 'People seem to think it had a bad effect on you and after that you started seeing a lot of women, but you were never serious about any of them.'

He pulled a face. 'You don't want to believe everything you hear…although I will say there was a bit of a trust issue after what happened with Rosa.'

'Oh, yes. I can empathize with that,' she said with feeling. 'And yet…you named your boat after her. Have you never wanted to paint over the name *Bella Rosa*?'

'No, no…' He laughed. 'You have it all wrong, *querida*. Rosa is my mother's name. I named the boat after her. Hers is a memory I will treasure for ever.'

'Oh…' She gasped. 'All this time I've been thinking—'

'You've been thinking of two and two and coming up with five. As for Mattie's father, Rosa's husband, I heard he's on his way to the hospital to be with both of them. He's a sailor, and he was on board ship, but he managed to get compassionate leave to be at his son's side. Unfortunately, things took a little longer than expected.'

'Do you think they'll get back together?'

'I think so. He loves her. They'll sort something out.'

He studied her thoughtfully for a second or two. 'How could you think Mattie was my son? Do you really think I would abandon my own child?'

'I don't know… Sometimes these things happen.'

'Never. Not to me. I would never leave my child.'

She smiled at him, relief coursing through her. 'So you do want children of your own one day?'

He folded her into his arms and looked into her eyes. 'Oh, yes, *querida*…as long as they are yours and mine. I love you, Jessie. Don't you know that? I think I've loved you almost from the start, but I couldn't believe what was happening to me. I've never fallen for any woman the way I fell for you. I want to be with you, to keep you by my side always. Do you think you could ever feel the same way about me?'

'Oh, yes. I've fallen in love with you, too, José. I tried not to let it happen…I tried so hard, but somehow you managed to sneak through my defences, and after that I was lost. I didn't want to be, but I realized I was hopelessly, head over heels in love with you. And then the worst happened and I thought I was losing you.'

'Believe me, that's never going to happen.' He kissed her tenderly, and she wound her arms around him and clung to him, giving herself up to that heavenly embrace. He was her dream come true, his love a magical paradise island fantasy that had turned out to be the real thing. She was the happiest woman in the world.

'I'm glad,' he said softly.

She looked up at him, her mind lost in a mist of desire. 'Did I say it aloud?'

'You did. You said you're the happiest woman in the world, and I'm really glad you feel that way. There's only one thing that can make life any better right now.'

'What's that?'

'You…giving me the right answer to my question…'

'And that is…?'

'Jessie, will you marry me?'

'Oh, yes…yes.'

He kissed her again. 'And now I'm the luckiest man in the world.' He smiled down at her. 'My grandparents will be so pleased. They think the world of you.'

'I think they're pretty much okay, too.' She ran her fingers lightly over his jaw. 'You know, you're going to have to take on the plantation—you can't let your grandfather fret about it any longer.'

He chuckled. 'He said you would talk to me and make me see sense. And, look, already you've sorted out what needs to be done.' He dropped a kiss on to her waiting lips. 'I'll install a plantation manager and keep an eye on things from afar. Do you think that will do?'

'I think it's perfect,' she said softly. 'So we don't need to worry about anything at all, do we? So now will you kiss me again…please?'

* * * * *

MILLS & BOON®

Classic romances from your favourite authors!

3 in 1 GREAT VALUE

40% OFF!

The Jarrods: Temptation

MAUREEN CHILD — TESSA RADLEY — KATHIE DENOSKY

By Request

The Australian's Desire

MARION LENNOX — LILIAN DARCY

By Request

Royal and Ruthless

ROBYN DONALD — ANNIE WEST — CHRISTINA HOLLIS

By Request

Whether you love tycoon billionaires, rugged ranchers or dashing doctors, this collection has something to suit everyone this New Year. Plus, we're giving you a huge 40% off the RRP!

Hurry, order yours today at
www.millsandboon.co.uk/NYCollection

0215_INSHIP2

MILLS & BOON®

Two superb collections!

40% OFF!

Would you rather spend the night with a seductive sheikh or be whisked away to a tropical Hawaiian island? Well, now you don't have to choose! Get your hands on both collections today and get 40% off the RRP!

Hurry, order yours today at
www.millsandboon.co.uk/TheOneCollection

215_INSHIP1

MILLS & BOON®

First Time in Forever

Following the success of the Snow Crystal trilogy, Sarah Morgan returns with the sensational Puffin Island trilogy. Follow the life, loss and love of Emily Armstrong in the first instalment, as she looks for love on Puffin Island.

Pick up your copy today!

Visit
www.millsandboon.co.uk/Firsttime

0215_ST_8

MILLS & BOON®

Why not subscribe?
Never miss a title and save money too!

Here's what's available to you if you join the
exclusive **Mills & Boon Book Club** today:

✦ *Titles up to a month ahead of the shops*
✦ *Amazing discounts*
✦ *Free P&P*
✦ *Earn Bonus Book points that can be redeemed*
  against other titles and gifts
✦ *Choose from monthly or pre-paid plans*

Still want more?
Well, if you join today we'll even give you
50% OFF your first parcel!

So visit **www.millsandboon.co.uk/subs**
or call Customer Relations on **020 8288 2888**
to be a part of this exclusive Book Club!

BS_2014

MILLS & BOON®

MEDICAL ROMANCE™

THE ULTIMATE IN ROMANTIC MEDICAL DRAMA

A sneak peek at next month's titles...

In stores from 6th March 2015:

- **Baby Twins to Bind Them** – Carol Marinelli *and*
  The Firefighter to Heal Her Heart – Annie O'Neil

- **Tortured by Her Touch** – Dianne Drake *and*
  It Happened in Vegas – Amy Ruttan

- **The Family She Needs** – Sue MacKay
- **A Father for Poppy** – Abigail Gordon

Available at WHSmith, Tesco, Asda, Eason, Amazon and Apple

Just can't wait?
Buy our books online a month before they hit the shops!
visit www.millsandboon.co.uk

These books are also available in eBook format!

0215/03